D1798964

HEIRS

OF

AVALON

THE OUTLAWED
COLONIES -BOOK 2

GAIL DALEY

GAIL DALEY

GAIL'S OTHER BOOKS

SPACE COLONY JOURNALS

Options of Survival
Destiny Rising
Tomorrows Legacy
The Interstellar Jewel Heist
The Designer People
Alien Trails
Quantum Light
Soturi*
Confederation Planets & People

PORTAL WORLD TALES

Portal World Notes (St. Antoni & the
Outlaw Colonies)
Rulari—Land of Myth & Magic

ST. ANTONI - THE FORBIDDEN

COLONY

Warriors of St. Antoni
The Enforcers
The Gaslight Bandits
The Portal Lawman
Cradle of Fire
The Clone Initiative

THE OUTLAWED COLONIES

Game Theory
Heirs of Avalon
Apex Predator
Babylon Shattered*

Cloned Ambition*

MAGI OF RULARI

Spell of The Magi
Magi Storm
Paladin

NON-FICTION

The Complete Modern Artist's Handbook

PAMPHLETS

Introduction to The Internet #1
The Hard Stuff - Handbook #2
Art Show Basics - Handbook #3
Framing on a Budget - Handbook #4
Are You Making Money? - Handbook #5
Just For Writers - Handbook #6*

*Working Title. Release dates TBA

HEIRS OF AVALON — BOOK 2 THE OUTLAW COLONIES

e-Book ISBN: 978-1-68564-021-7
Print ISBN- 978-1-68564-024-8
HB ISBN; 978-1-68489-196-2
ASIN:

For permission requests, write to the publisher, addressed "Attention: Permissions Coordinator," at the address below.

Gail Daley
5688 E Sussex Way
Fresno, CA 93727
www.gaildaley.com

Ordering Information: Quantity sales. Special discounts are available on quantity purchases by corporations, associations, and others. For details, contact the "Bulk Sales Department" at the address above.

The name Barsoom which is used as the name of a colony in these books, BARSOOM(R) is a registered trademark of Edgar Rice Burroughs, Inc. And Used by Permission.

GAIL DALEY

ABOUT THIS BOOK

Stolen Technology sparks a Murder

A Futuristic Science Fiction Thriller

The theft Top Secret technology is the catalyst for a lab tech's murder and plunges two couples into a web of criminal activity

Two couples from different worlds search for stolen technology while working to uncover a murderer

Returning home to Barsoom after a successful mission to earth, Randal brings an unexpected dividend with him: A data crystal with the formula for finding earth-type planets. When the data crystal is stolen and a lab tech murdered during the break-in, his father and his fiancée's father come under suspicion. It's up to him, his fiancée Judith, and some new friends to clear their fathers of murder and find and retrieve the stolen crystal before it falls into the wrong hands.

The name Barsoom which is used as the name of a colony in these books, BARSOOM(R) is a registered trademark of Edgar Rice Burroughs, Inc. And Used by Permission.

GAIL DALEY

Table of Contents

HARMONIC PORTAL

DEVON LOOKED up from his terminal with a welcoming smile as Tash Higgins walked in the door.

Tash was worth looking at. She was about medium height for a woman, with straight, blue-black hair pulled back in a ponytail, an exquisitely sculpted face and a lush figure that would make any red-blooded man sit up and take notice. Devon fell into that category; he had been in love with her since the first day he met her nearly thirteen years ago.

He was painfully aware she regarded him only as a friend. He knew he didn't have vid-hero looks. His ordinary features and limp brown hair certainly didn't rate a second glance from most women, and since he dressed for comfort rather than style, his loose pants and shirt concealed the hard muscles he had been at pains to develop ever since he realized his scholarly/scientific interests made him a target for school bullies. As an adult, he kept in shape by training with the Blue Moon Militia, the local militia group which kept the town of Laughing Mountain and the area around it safe from infringement of their rights by the state and national governments who ruled most of North America.

"Did the mail pouches come in?" he asked, referring to mail pouches from the illegal colonies who used the town of Laughing Mountain to funnel goods and services to earth and to each other. The colonies and the Portal who serviced them were illegal because neither Earth-Gov nor the Industrial Giants who ruled behind the scenes had given permission for them to exist. For a variety of reasons, chief among them being a dislike of conforming to someone else's rules, the colonies of St. Antoni, Barsoom, Arcadia, Shangri-La and Halcyon had been developed in defiance of the two entities who ruled post-apocalyptic earth. The town of Laughing Mountain, who had built the illegal portal to access them, sponsored the colonies out of economic necessity.

Desperate for operating funds after a series of pandemics and global-wide earthquakes had devastated the planet, Laughing Mountain's economic base as an event town had been in deep financial trouble when Earth-Gov announced it would hold a lottery for places to develop the portals to new worlds. Towns were invited to submit applications. Laughing Mountain wasn't lucky enough to win a spot, but economic necessity forced them to go ahead anyway. A Portal was created in defiance of the draconian laws against operating an unregulated Portal.

"Yes, the pouches came in. That's partly what I wanted to talk to you about," she said.

"Flattery will get you anywhere," he told her with a smile.

"Both Tally and Ivette sent letters and photos of the children and asked me to make sure Scarlet Jones gets a copy. I was hoping I could tag along the next time you went out to the Phoenix Spa."

The Phoenix Spa was an abandoned resort purchased through channels by Napoleon Bonaparte the leader of the free clones. He had arranged for Devon to build a portal generator and blackmailed the clone industry into financing the colony, by agreeing to cease destroying their clone farms.

Devon and Tash had first met Scarlet Jones when they were in

college. The group of students they
hung with had discovered a clone farm
in the hills above the town of San
Demos when they followed a group of
male students there. Scarlet had been
recently sold to the farm when her
former owner died. Furious at being
forced to serve as a whore, she had
broken free and run for the
electrified fence enclosing the
property. Liam Brendan, Tash's
brother-in-law to be, had fired into
the transformer box electrifying the
fence. The shot had blown out the
power to the complex, allowing
Scarlet to escape. The group had
taken her in and helped her to reach
her mate, Dagmar Ironroar, and his
group of escaped clones. After she
had left to find her friends, Tash
and the others had discovered someone
had murdered most of the inhabitants
of the farm. They went in to search
for survivors and found seven
abandoned toddlers alone and

starving. Ivette Hayes who was from Arcadia and her husband Mathias had adopted them. Tash's sister Tally had been in another room when six of the artificial wombs used to breed clones had decanted six babies. When the group left the complex, they had taken all the children with them.

A second encounter with Scarlet and Dagmar hadn't been as friendly; they had broken into Liam's house to rescue the cloned babies because they feared what the 'Normals' intended to do with them. During the battle, Hogun Silverhorn, Dagmar's second in command, had been wounded by Randal Langton a student from Barsoom. Barely escaping after losing the fight, Dagmar and the others had traveled to the Phoenix Spa to get medical help for Hogun.

The Phoenix Spa was the location where Napoleon, the Free Clones defacto leader had established his headquarters. Once a destination for the rich and famous, it had gone out of business during the disasters and lain deserted until Napoleon had managed to purchase it through a subsidiary company to disguise his identity. He had recently hired Devon to develop a Portal for the new colony of Halcyon, where he intended to establish a clone colony. In consequence, Devon made regular trips to the Spa to check on the progress of the portal.

"You're always welcome to come with me," Devon said, "you know that."

"Thank you," she said. "Would you like to see what Tally and Ivette sent?"

"Did you open the letters too?"

"Of course not," she said indignantly. "The family got duplicates of the pictures and letters."

She set the pouch she carried on a nearby desk and took out the set of

folding framed oil paintings Tally had sent, opening it out to show the six babies.

"These are really good," Devon said. "They look professional. Who did them?"

"Liam's sister Jade is an artist," Tash said. "She did one set for Liam and Tally as a wedding present. Tally liked them so much she asked for copies for us and Scarlet."

Ivette had sent something different; an eight-sided holo cube. Seven of the sections featured each of the toddlers in various activities, and the eighth was a base where it sat.

When Tash touched it, it projected a holo vid of each of the children in turn. "Wow," Devon said, his professional curiosity aroused. "I wonder how this was made."

Tash made a rude sound. "If that isn't just like you—wondering about

how it was made, instead of looking
at the kids!"

He grinned at the reprimand.
"That's me—a born nerd."

"When do you leave for the spa?"

"Day after tomorrow. I'm waiting
for a part to come in. Can you be
ready by then?"

"Yes," she said. "When will you
find them a planet?"

"Oh, we've found one. Mark Connors
Dad has been allowing us to run the
search program in the early mornings
during the week."

She frowned. "I thought he was
afraid having the Portal generator
under power would attract attention
from Portal Authority agents."

"We've been running it about 3
AM," he said. "Commander Malachi
agreed to do extra militia patrols
during that time. After his people
rousted a couple of agents out of the
woods, they pretty much backed off."
He grinned. "When the Portal

Authority complained, Commander Sullivan told Agent Thomas the militia was doing night training and would be active in the area for the next couple of weeks. Plus, Sheriff Gonzalez had his officers threaten to tow any cars he found parked at deserted properties and charge the owners with trespass."

"What's the new planet like?" she asked.

"A little like St. Antoni," he said. "Geologically it's in the Pleistocene era. The Portal will be on the coast in the northern continent. We tested the soil, and it will grow human food, so that means the animals there will be compatible with human digestion. It's got broadleaf forests in the southern half of the Northern continents, plenty of rivers and streams. It also has prairies, valleys, and deserts. The drone map found large herds of herbivories, some of which can probably be tamed for food or riding animals. The oceans are salty, although less so than those on earth, and there seems to be an abundant number of fish and crustaceans. No monster sized predators the way we found on Lemuria—at least the drones didn't find any."

"A new world," she said with a sigh. "I'd love to see all of them, and to visit there…"

"I seem to have been elected as the Outlaw Portal expert, so I'll probably visit all of them sooner or later. I could use an assistant. Interested in a job?"

"I'm not a programmer or a techie. What would I be doing?"

"Personal contact with clients. I'm no good at it, and it takes time away from working on the Portals."

"You've got yourself an assistant. Oh, I guess I should have asked. What does the job pay?"

Devon burst out laughing. "I draw a pretty good chunk of change for what I do, so since you'll be relieving me of customer relations how does this sound?" He named a figure that had her mouth dropping open.

"You can afford to pay that much to an assistant?"

"Yes," he said. "And I do need someone to run interference with the locals while I work on programming and repairs."

A BIBLICAL LESSON

THE PHOENIX SPA was south of the town of San Demos, along what was left of the California Coast. The erupting volcanos and earthquakes had decimated a once prosperous area, and when half the coast range slid into the ocean, many high-end resorts catering to the rich and famous had simply been abandoned.

When Devon and Tash arrived at the wrought iron gates, she simply stared. Beyond the gate, with is leaping Phoenix rising from the flames, she could see masses of weed-covered overgrown sidewalks and dead grass. Devon pushed a remote button and the heavy gates swung outward. The area leading to the hotel had once been a carefully tended park with flowers, fountains, and sculptured walkways. Now the flowers, although still beautiful ran wild. The fountains held pools of stagnant water and the sculptured walks were overgrown with weeds.

The four-story red brick structure at the end of the drive was thick with ivy. The once white columns supporting the roof were stained and cracked. The graceful marble steps leading to the porch were no longer white; time had yellowed them as it had the porch.

"It looks like something out of a horror vid," Tash said.

"A little," Devon agreed. "But please don't say so, Napoleon is quite proud of it."

He parked the van in front of the Spa and went around back to unload the parts boxes onto a small wrought iron cart.

A tall, silver haired man descended the steps.

"Morton," he said by way of greeting. "You know we don't allow strangers here. Who is this?"

"Yael, this is Tash Higgins, my assistant," Devon replied. "Tash this is Yael, Napoleon's second in command."

"Hello," Tash said, with a smile. "I'm pleased to meet you."

Yael ignored her. "You didn't mention an assistant before this."

"I hired Tash for her customer relation skills," Devon replied. "I realized the work would proceed faster if I didn't have to stop and chit-chat with customers."

"I see," Yael said. "Does Ms. Higgins know we don't discuss our location with anyone?"

"Yes, I do," Tash said. "We never discuss Portal locations, or any business done with outlawed colonies. If you'll grab the other end of the cart we can take these parts inside, and Devon can install them."

Anderez scowled, but he grabbed the other end of the wire cart as requested and Devon followed him up the stairs.

Tash looked around her with interest when they entered what used to be the lobby of the hotel, a wide triangle shaped room with tall, stained-glass windows. The late afternoon sun created colorful kaleidoscope patterns on the white marble floor. At the far end of the room sat an elevated gazebo. The man who occupied it was a sight to behold. He was tall, with broad shoulders, a flat abdomen and long, muscled legs. His sculptured features were barely blunted enough to keep him from being classed as pretty. Tash studied him as they walked toward him. There was strength there, coupled with the arrogance of a man who was used to getting his own way.

For some reason she was reminded of the late Dan Simmons, the man who had stalked her older sister and was indirectly responsible for her and her sisters moving to Laughing Mountain.

"Napoleon, this is my assistant, Tash Higgins," Devon said when they halted below the steps of the Gazabo.

"You are fortunate in finding such a lovely woman to assist you," Napoleon's voice was a warm baritone. "Welcome to Phoenix, Ms. Higgins."

"Thank you," Tash said. "I've been looking forward to seeing it."

"I take it the part came in?" Napoleon addressed Devon.

"Yes, I have it with me. If the structure to contain the Portal is complete, we can activate it as soon as I get it installed. Tash and I will need to go across to install a similar one on the Halcyon generator."

"The construction is almost finished," Yael said. "We were delayed because the mortar wasn't curing properly," he explained to Napoleon.

"If you will excuse us, I'd like to take a look at what you've accomplished," Devon said.

"Certainly," Napoleon replied.

"Is Scarlet Jones in residence?" Tash asked. "I have letters and gifts from my sister Tally and Ivette Hayes-Bedingfeld for her."

"I believe she is teaching a class on how to blend into human society," Yael answered. "If you'll come with me, I'll show you to the classroom. It should be almost finished."

"Great!" Tash said. She went to the cart and retrieved a canvas tote.

One of Tash's strengths, due to her keen observation skills, was her ability to judge people and she caught the faint frown on Napoleon's face as Yael led her away.

"The crucial keynote to blending into human society is believing you are their equals," Scarlet was saying as Tash and Yael stepped into the room. "I believe the solution to acquiring that belief is through the doctrine of the Clone Familia movement."

One of the men raised a hand. "Why do you think the movement is so important?"

"A good question. Humans or Normals who create clones take away much of the things necessary for everyone to develop a healthy self-respect and confidence. Please read the material for your next class when we will discuss its implications."

Scarlet was a tall blond with a superb figure and finely boned features. She had been a special commission for an actress who intended to have her brain transplanted into the body when Scarlet reached maturity.

Fortunately for Scarlet, the old woman had suffered an aneurism and died before that could happen.

While she was waiting for Scarlet to mature, the old actress had rented Scarlet's services to a film company who had also rented some clone cage fighters to ensure the fight scenes in the movie were realistic. It was during the filming Scarlet had met Dagmar Ironroar and the two had become mates.

Tash sat in one of the chairs in the back of the room as Scarlet dismissed the class.

When Scarlet came to greet them, Yael met her with a frown.

"Didn't Napoleon tell you he doesn't approve the Clone Familia doctrine?"

"I believe that is short-sighted of him," Scarlet replied. "A belief in themselves as a worthy individual is essential for clones who go into Normals society. The best way to develop that belief is through the Clone Familia doctrine."

"I'll have to report this to him," Yael told her.

"You must do whatever your duties to him requires," Scarlet replied, unmoved.

"You have a visitor from Laughing Mountain, Tash Higgins," Yael told her.

"Yes, thank you Yael."

"My sister and Ivette sent letters and pictures of the children," Tash said, lifting the tote.

"Wonderful!" Scarlet exclaimed. "Let's go to my apartment and have a cup of tea. I don't have another class until this evening."

Yael watched them go. He would have preferred to see and hear what they were going to discuss but obviously, Scarlet wanted privacy to hear what Tash had to say. Napoleon would want to know as well.

He was aware Napoleon's plans for Scarlet didn't include her having allies who might help her if she defied him. Napoleon made a habit of co-opting any female clone he took a fancy to for sex. Most of them had been flattered and willing. The few who hadn't—better not to think about that.

Scarlet's apartment was simple, consisting of a bedroom/sitting area with an attached bathroom.

When they arrived, she gestured for Tash to set the Tote on a chair and filled a glass carafe with water which she heated in an old-fashioned microwave.

While she fussed with the tea things, Tash drew the two gifts out of the tote and laid the letters on the table beside them.

"So, you are teaching acclimation classes," she remarked. "What is Dagmar doing?"

A shadow crossed Scarlet's face.
"Napoleon sent him and the others on
a scouting expedition to Halcyon.
That was two months ago. I haven't
heard from him since."

"Devon intends for us to go across
and check on the equipment on the
Halcyon side once he gets the Portal
running on this end. Why don't you go
with us?"

Scarlet put her face in her hands
and burst into tears. "Maybe he won't
be glad to see me."

Tash set down her cup and rose to
put her arms around the other woman.
"It's going to be okay," she said,
patting Scarlet comfortingly on the
back. "Why wouldn't he want to see
you?"

Scarlet wiped her eyes with the
tissue Tash handed her. "I think
Napoleon sent him away so he could
have access to me. He's been very
attentive since Dagmar has been gone.
I keep wondering if Dagmar agreed to

an arrangement about it and that's why he hasn't contacted me."

"If that's the case, you *have* to come with us. It's better to know, than to guess, isn't it?"

Scarlet straightened her spine. "You're right." In an obvious move to change the subject, she asked, "What did Tally and Ivette send me?"

Tash unwrapped the cloth covered oil paintings first. "The artist is Jade Brendan, Tally's sister-in-law. She connected two sets of 5 x 7 triptych frames to make a set of six. Each portrait has the baby's name under it."

"These are wonderful! I can keep these?"

"Yes, of course. She also sent another set to Joyce."

"They are so lifelike."

Tash watched as Scarlet ran a finger over each of the children's names.

"Ivette sent you something as well." Tash unfolded the cloth protecting the hologram. "Touch it and it projects a holo vid of each of the toddlers."

Gingerly, Scarlet reached out to touch the cube. "Immediately a holo of a toddler appeared. "Hi, Aunt Scarlet," it said. "I'm Leonardo Hayes-Bedlingfeld. I like to swing." The holo changed to a vid of Leo on the swing set. Rafe and Don showed off their tumbling skills, Fran and Daphne sang, Gabe was sculpting a figure out of clay and Jillian was playing with Rika, her vole.

Scarlet was forced to wipe her eyes again. "They look so happy," she said.

"I believe they are," Tash said. "If you want to write them thank you notes, I can make sure the letters get sent back through the mail pouches." She tapped the two unopened letters. "We got letters from them too. They both asked how you are doing, so I know they will appreciate hearing from you."

FAREWELLS & NEW BEGINNINGS

"ARE YOU SURE you won't change your mind and come with us?" Tash asked Scarlet when they said goodbye.

"Thank you, but no. Now that I've spoken to Dagmar, I know what to tell Napoleon if he summons me to his bed," Scarlet said. "It's possible we might need to leave Phoenix though. In that case I hope I can count on you to help us emigrate to one of the other colonies."

"Of course. Joyce and Tam will always know how to get in touch with me," Tash replied.

She and Scarlet exchanged hugs before Tash and Devon departed. Yael watched them from the top of the steps.

"What was that about?" Devon inquired.

Tash was silent, considering what to tell him. "How good is your bible knowledge?" she asked.

"About as good as anyone's, I guess. What does that have to do with what you and Scarlet were discussing?"

"Do you remember the story of David and Bathsheba?"

"Wasn't he a king in Israel or something?"

"Yes. The story goes, he saw Bathsheba taking a bath on her rooftop and decided he wanted her, but she was married. Her husband was off fighting a war. David sent for her, raped her, and sent her home. The rape created a child. He wasn't in love with her, she was a

'disposable' person to him. He
murdered her husband to hide his sin
and forced her to marry him. God
punished him anyway—the baby died."

"Okay. I'm still waiting for the
punchline."

"Napoleon wants Scarlet. He sent
Dagmar off on that scouting
expedition to get him out of the way
while he tries to court Scarlet."

"Does Dagmar know about this?"

"He does now. He didn't realize
Scarlet wasn't getting any of his
letters. She was beginning to think
he was willing to give her up to
Napoleon."

"That sucks."

"Big time. Apparently, the six of
them have joined a movement called
the Clone Familia. She seems to think
it might protect her from Napoleon."

"I don't know," Devon said slowly.
"The first week I was here, one of
the male clones issued a challenge to
another one because he wanted his

woman. They fought, and the woman didn't seem to have much to say about it."

"According to Scarlet, if Napoleon tries that, she will declare she refuses to accept the results of the challenge."

"Can she do that?"

"I don't know. I know much about clone culture."

Devon was silent during the rest of the drive back to Laughing Mountain. He pulled into the drive behind the office he shared with Jase.

"I wonder," he said.

"About what?" Tash inquired.

"I'm wondering if we might send Dagmar the parts to make a second portal. One that isn't under Napoleon's control."

"How would you keep him or Yael from finding out about it?"

"I'm not sure yet."

"Where do we go next?"

"The next Portal weekend is the Renaissance Fair, isn't it? Randal needs to get the data crystal I made for him back home, so he'll be returning with us."

"Any special clothes I should take?"

"The kind of stuff you'd wear if you were in period for a renaissance play, I guess."

Randal Langeton was waiting for them in the office. Randal had come to earth to learn Portal technology, and to implant a virus into the PA's data base to block its search engines from discovering any of the colonies connected to Laughing Mountain. He was about Devon's height, a slim, hard muscled man, with dark auburn hair. He was also a master bladesman, an expert with the saber, rapier, and epee as well as other renaissance weapons popular during that period on earth.

The Office Devon shared with Jase Delaney, who handled most of the E-work needed to keep the town and visitors from the colonies off the Portal Authorities radar, was still open although it was late afternoon. Jase was a few years older than Devon and Tash. He was engaged to her sister Tam who was majoring in Law at the University. They planned to get married when she passed the bar exam.

Tash had once had a crush on Jase, but it had ended when she realized how much he and her sister loved each other. Only Devon knew the night she had realized Jase and Tam were an item was the night she had planned to seduce Jase.

Devon had followed her when she had fled into the forest to sob out her heartbreak and embarrassment. He hadn't said anything, just handed her a bottle of water to sooth her throat. She had always been grateful for his kindness that night.

That night after dinner, Tam came to watch Tash pack for Barsoom. "I hear it's hot there; maybe you better take some shorts and tank tops," she suggested.

"Randal says they all wear long sleeves and pants made of thin cotton. Because it's in the tropic zone, they have lots of bugs. Not looking forward to that."

"Ick," Tam shuddered. "I remember those huge beetles we found in that first apartment, nasty." She hesitated, watching her sister. "Tash, you aren't doing this to get away from Jase and me, are you?"

"No, I'm looking forward to seeing all these new planets. Imagine—a entire new world, just waiting to be explored, and I'm lucky enough to be able to see five of them!"

"Well, okay. You know I have a few blouses I can lend you to take with you."

"Which ones?" Tash asked warily. The girls were part of three identical triplets so she knew any of Tam's clothes would fit her. However, they had quite different tastes in fashion.

"C'mon, let's go choose," Tam said, dragging her off to her room.

Watching them, Joyce rocked one of her twin sons while Mark changed the other.

"I'm glad to see that," she told him. "I don't have to tell you I was worried about them. Tally was always the balance wheel, and for both of them to fall for the same guy…"

Mark blew a raspberry on his son's tummy, causing the baby to giggle and kick. "I'm glad she'll be traveling with Devon and Randal," he said. "They'll look after her."

AN ISLE UNKNOWN

LAUGHING MOUNTAIN disguised their Portal entry as a stone arch. When a wedding was being held in the center, the arch was festooned with paper bridal bells, flowers, and sometimes huge bows. Other events also decorated it. During a Portal run, it filled with swirling color as carts bearing loaded wagons traversed the passageway between Earth and Barsoom.

Tash and Devon rode through the Portal to Barsoom with Randal. Devon and Randal had both made the trip before, so other than to note the passage, they paid relatively little attention to what was happening. For

Tash it was still a new experience. The absolute silence when they entered was eerie. She found herself holding her breath, despite knowing they wouldn't be in transition long enough for the lack of air to matter.

When she and Devon had crossed into Halcyon, they had come out on a bare landscape of sand dunes. Behind them the surf pounded on the shore and strange sea birds screamed at each other. The air had been crisp with the tang of sea salt.

Crossing into Barsoom was different. The air here was uncomfortably humid, and she could feel her underarms growing damp. Because the colonists had made efforts to retain the look and feel of their new planet, they hadn't tried to clear out the flora to make room for all the transports needed for shipping products to and from earth. In consequence the portal was surrounded by a tropical rain forest.

Immensely tall trees, with their broad, flat leaves stretching upward, blocked out much of the sunlight. It was noisy; tropical bird songs caroled by colorful singers filled the atmosphere with trilling music. The scents of large, perfumed flowers clogged the air. Occasionally the sound of a predatory growl echoed from the jungle.

The Portal itself had a gently sloping roof made of water-resistant plasticrete tiles. The gate itself was wide and tall enough so Tash thought three or four semi-trucks could have driven through it. The floor resembled cobblestone and was rough enough to help prevent slippage if it got wet, which it frequently did. Outside the Portal itself was a staging area filled with old-fashioned looking wooden wagons. Like much of the tech on Barsoom, the wagons weren't as old-fashioned as they looked; in the front of each driver's bench was a console with gears and a steering wheel. When one of Laughing Mountains golf carts tied into it to take it into the Portal, the console folded neatly into the front of the wagon.

"Does anyone know we're coming?" Devon asked Randal.

"I commed Judith, but I don't know if—"

"I'm here," a woman's voice said.

Tash turned and found herself confronting a tiny, flame-haired fairy who regarded her with a slightly hostile gaze. The girl in front of her although tiny in statue, had been endowed by nature with a Rubenesque figure. Her bright red hair was anchored under a wide-brimmed hat with an enormous feather. She had a small animal tucked under one arm.

"Hello," Tash said with a smile. "I'm Tash Higgins. I'm Devon's assistant."

"I'm Judith Garneys, Randal's fiancée," was the response.

"Randal didn't tell us about you. I'm pleased to meet you, Judith." Tash knew her height and looks sometimes intimidated other women. Coupled with Randal's luke-warm greeting to his fiancé, the reason for the hostility was obvious. Judith most likely thought Tash's presence was due to Randal.

Randal, evidently perceiving an issue, although not sure what it was, said hastily, "It's good to see you looking so well, Judith."

This was a little unfortunate, as it caused Judith to stiffen and glare at him. "Oh, and I looked so bad before that anything is an improvement?"

"No, of course not! I didn't mean—" he looked around desperately for inspiration and found it in the animal Judith was holding under one arm.

"I see you still have Licorice. How old is he now?"

"He's two," Judith replied.

"Oh," Tash exclaimed. "What is it? Its adorable."

"This is Licorice," Judith said, her expression softening. She shifted her pet so Tash could see him better. Licorice was about the size of an earthly Guinea Pig. He looked hairless, but his wrinkly skin was covered by fine, nearly transparent hair. His large, bat-like ears stuck out on either side of his head, and big almond shaped eyes regarded Tash with interest. "We call them Catamounts. He's native to Barsoom."

Tash held out a finger for Licorice to sniff. He did so and made a chuffing sound.

"He likes you," Judith said in surprise. "He doesn't warm up to most people, but he likes you."

"We have lots of pets at home," Tash said. "Maybe he smells them on me. I miss them. Before Tally got married and moved to St. Antoni, she seemed to bring home a stray animal every other week."

"Did you bring a transport?" Randal asked Judith. "Devon has a lot of equipment."

"I have the family carriage," Judith replied. "It's over here." She led the way to what seemed to be a horse-drawn carriage, minus the horses. A robot driver dressed in livery sat on the driver's box. Opening the door, she climbed inside, and Tash followed her, while Randal and Devon loaded the baggage on the roof and the boot in the rear of the carriage.

"No robot horses?" Tash inquired.

Judith shrugged. "Some families have them, but they are only for show. These things run on Gregor Crystals."

When Randal and Devon climbed inside, Randal ordered the carriage to go to his parents' house.

"You and Tash will be staying with us," he told Devon. "We'll get your bags unloaded and you settled in your rooms and then you and I can take the new data crystal over to the lab."

Tash eyed him thoughtfully. "Ah— do your parents know you're bringing guests?"

Randal looked at Judith. "Did you tell them?"

"Since you didn't tell *me*, the answer is no," she retorted.

"It doesn't matter, we always have room," Randal said. Tash noticed he did tap his com to let his mother know he was bringing home guests.

The Capital city of Savano was a city of subtly and deception. Much of the houses and buildings looked as if they could have been transplanted from a country village in Europe. However, looks can be deceiving;

Barsoomians were too fond of techy
gadgets to give up modern
conveniences. Like the Portal
Terminal, the capital city of Savano
was surrounded by the rainforest much
of which had been left intact. The
buildings were interspersed among the
towering trees in such a way
travelers often didn't see them until
they were quite near. Because it
rained so much (every other day) to
prevent flooding, the houses had
stilt foundations below the first
floors. An octogen shape had been
adapted for most of the buildings as
the design provided light, air and
spectacular views.

Ordinarily Tash would have asked
loads of questions about Judith's
engagement and wedding plans but
considering the girl and Randal
didn't seem on good terms, she didn't
think it was a good idea. She
searched her mind for a neutral topic
and found it in Judith's pet. "Does

everyone have a catamount for a pet?" she asked.

"A few of us like myself have always had them, but it became fashionable recently to have one with you."

"What happens when it stops being fashionable?" Tash inquired.

"I suppose other people will pass them on to younger siblings."

"Is that what you will do?"

"No," Judith said, stroking Licorice. "He's mine for life. I suppose I could stop taking him everywhere with me, but I don't intend to do that either."

"I'm glad. Tally used to get so angry when the students at college would adopt a pet and then throw them away when it came time to go home. A bunch of them were dumpster rescues."

"They just threw them away?" Judith was horrified.

"Yeah. Some people are—"

"Cruel and horrible," Judith finished.

"Yes," Tash agreed.

"Your sister sounds like a nice person. You say she recently got married and moved away?"

Tash chuckled. "Yes, but before she left, she and her new husband adopted six clone infants. Liam is from St. Antoni. He said they would merely be kids there, so she agreed to move off planet even if it meant not seeing the family much."

"Aren't they only kids on earth as well?"

"Unfortunately, no," Devon said. "Clone rights are a controversial subject on Earth. The Clone makers claim they are the property of whoever created them. There are also two opposing groups—one of which wants clones given full human rights, and the other declares they are abominations and should be destroyed. Liam and Tally's babies will be much

safer on St. Antoni; so, will the toddlers Mathias and Ivette took back to Arcadia."

Randal's home was a three-story building. The first floor was set on stilts making it about two foot off the ground, Since Barsoom was a rainy planet whose rivers and streams periodically overflowed their banks, most buildings on Barsoom were Octagon shaped and built on stilts to avoid damage by the frequent floods.

The house had a wrap-around porch on all sides. A secondary attached building apparently held air sleds. When they arrived, two robo servers in footman's livery came out to unload the baggage and Devon's equipment.

Randal's mother was a short, middle-aged woman with cropped grey hair. She greeted her son with hugs and tears, scolding him for being gone so long. When Randal introduced Devon and Tash, she greeted them warmly, apologizing for not having their rooms ready for them.

"He didn't tell you we were coming, did he?" Tash asked with an understanding smile.

"Well, no, but he has such an important job, he doesn't always remember household things," Allison Langeton excused Randal. "Your father is coming home from the lab for lunch. He should be here any moment. You will stay and eat with us won't you Judith?"

"Yes, of course," Judith agreed.

Tash observed that whatever her differences with her fiancé might be, it was obvious Judith was on excellent terms with her mother-in-law to be.

Randal's father was a slim, dark man. Like his son, he stayed in shape by constant sword practice. He brought his partners, Agustin Garneys, and Gamel Underhill, home with him as they were all anxious to

examine the data crystal Randal had brought. Judith's Dad was a tall, spare man with his daughters bright red hair, now frosted with white. The third partner, Gamel Underhill, was a rotund, dark-complected man with a merry smile.

Lunch was much more elaborate than either Tash or Devon was accustomed to, consisting of four courses served by livery dressed robots: a salad course followed by soup and a roasted bird of some sort. Desert was a rich fruit tart served with a highly spiced cheese.

Tash had eaten a healthy serving of salad before she realized a lot more food was about to be served, and she started taking miniscule portions. So did Devon. To her astonishment, the tiny Judith put away a good-sized portion of each course. *The girl must have the metabolism of a rabbit*, Tash thought.

*If I ate that way all the time, I'd
be as fat as a hog.*

OF MICE & MEN

JUDITH FROWNED at Randal when she realized he intended to return to the lab after dinner. "This is your first night back. We've been invited to a party at Terrence Donavon's this evening, and we're all going."

"Judith, Devon, and I need to work with Dad and Agustin on the information we brought back. It's important to get it running as soon as possible."

"But not tonight," she said firmly. "Everyone knows you brought guests back with you from Earth and everyone wants to meet Devon and Tash."

Correctly reading his refusal, she added, "If we don't introduce them

tonight, everyone will think
something is hokey and start spying
on you to find out what you're
doing."

Randal made a disgusted noise.
"Alright." He turned to
Devon, "I don't suppose you brought
party clothes with you?"

"Uh—what kind of party clothes?"
Tash asked cautiously.

"Let's go and see what you have,"
Judith said. "Randal, Devon's about
your size. See if some of your stuff
will fit him."

As Judith hauled Tash off to
inspect her clothing choices, Randal
rolled his eyes.

"She's right, dammit. I've been
away so long I've forgotten what it's
like here."

Devon regarded him curiously.
"What do you mean?"

"We didn't only copy the lifestyle
from the Renaissance," he was told.
"Unfortunately, that period in

history was rampant with plots and intrigues where everyone spied on each other. Be as vague as possible tonight when you're asked why you came."

Deciding Tash had nothing appropriate, Judith took her home with her where she found a dress in her older sister's closet to fit Tash. The ankle length overskirt was bright red, with an ultramarine panel in front. The low-cut top was of off-white linen, under a bright red vest, cinched tightly at the waist with gold cord. The blouse had two rows of puffy material at the top of the narrow sleeves. It was also cut much lower than Tash was used to. All three of the triplets had inherited full, well-developed busts; most of which was put on display in the gown.

"My goodness!" Tash exclaimed when she saw herself in Judith's full-length mirror. "I can't wear this—I'll fall out of it!"

"Nonsense!" Judith laughed. "You look much better than Ava did in it. The young men will all be falling over themselves to dance with you!"

The dress also had a built-in slit for a poniard. Traditionally, Judith told her the weapon was worn in a sheath on her thigh. When Judith offered the dagger and the sheath to Tash, the girl from earth looked at it in horror. "You think I'll need that?"

Judith shrugged, and showed Tash hers, which was fastened on her thigh. "It doesn't hurt to be prepared," she said.

"I'd probably cut myself with it," Tash told her. "I've never had any training in using a knife for defense. Most of my self-defense classes were in unarmed combat."

"In that case, I think we'll do without it," Judith said.

Devon's mouth fell open when he and Randal arrived to escort the girls to the party. Both young men wore the traditional linen shirt with its wide, billowing sleeves under a brightly colored Doublet. The knee length breeches, striped in contrasting colors were loose and roomy, tied off under the knees with a red cord. Under it they wore matching leggings. Randal also wore calf length boots. It had been decided Devon's own boots would serve. Randal was in green, and Devon was in bright yellow and indigo.

"Is that what you're wearing?" Devon asked, staring at the amount of flesh Tash's gown displayed.

Tash felt her face heating up. "Judith says everyone else will be wearing something this low-cut," she defended the gown.

"Yeah, but I'll bet most of them don't have your—ah—attributes either."

Randal choked on a laugh and turned it into a cough. Tash glared

at both young men and Judith rolled
her eyes.

"Very funny," Tash snapped. "I've
refrained from making remarks about
codpieces, Devon so you can just shut
up about how much boob I'm showing!"

Randal did lose it. He leaned
against the door and howled.

Devon glared at him. "It isn't
funny!" he said. "How would you like
it if Judith went out in public with
so much on display?"

Randal eyed Judith. They had been
engaged since they were both children
and he had always taken her
appearance for granted. This was the
first time in years he had really
looked at her and it dawned on him
that his fiancé was a beautiful
woman. Judith's dress was the same
style as Tash was wearing. It did
show of lot of creamy flesh above the
waist. Judith was almost as well-
endowed as Tash in some areas, and a
considerable amount of her breast was

also on display. Very nice it was too. An unfamiliar feeling of possessiveness hit him, and he suddenly understood how Devon felt.

Mrs. Garney's nodded to herself, satisfied. Randal was finally looking at her daughter the way a man looks at a desirable woman instead of his old childhood playmate.

"Devon," Judith said patiently, "If Tash wears a high-necked dress, everyone will think she's a Dowd. The other girls will tear her to pieces."

"I'm afraid she's right, Devon," Randal told him. "The girls who attend these affairs are like chickens. One who stands out as different will get pecked to death—"

"Randal Langeton! That is the most disgusting comparison I ever heard! Are you calling me a chicken?"

"Ah—of course not," Randal denied in haste. "You look beautiful."

"Yes, she does," Judith's father said. "Both Judith and Tash look lovely." He looked over at the man who was soon to be his son-in-law with a grin. "Better shut your mouth before you dig that hole any deeper, son. You're about to drown as it is."

"Quite right," Judith's mother agreed. She looked the two girls over with a maternal eye. "You both look lovely. Tash, I'll make you a present of the dress, if only to keep Ava from wearing it out in public again. It looks so much better on you. My daughter insisted on buying it, and she should *never* wear red!"

"Try telling her that," Judith said under her breath.

"Thank you," Tash said. "It's a beautiful gown. Please thank your daughter for me."

When Judith chose to sit with Tash rather than beside him, Randal knew he was still in trouble. They rode in style to the party in an airsled modified to resemble a renaissance carriage on the outside. The colonists had deliberately designed many things on Barsoom to seem old world on the outside but all cutting-edge tech inside.

The colonists had made every attempt to preserve the natural ambience of the Planet, so the Donovan's home was surrounded by a bioluminescent jungle of tall trees with large fronds. The Nightbirds called to each other and occasionally they could hear a predator roar and the squeal of its prey.

The robot driver dropped them off on the dock in front of the house and went to park in a nearby parking slot.

"I'm glad I don't have to try to park in that," Devon remarked, eying the narrow slit the robo driver slid the sled into. There were about ten rows of slots filled with sleds stacked on top of each other.

"It looks like a good crowd tonight," Judith said happily. "I didn't go out much while Randal was gone."

"Why not?" Tash asked her.

"Oh, well, some guys will misunderstand if an engaged girl goes to a party without her fiancé."

"Is there anything we should know not to do?" Devon asked.

"Keep an eye on your drink," Judith said as they entered the foyer. "Most of our crowd wouldn't put anything in it, but there's always a few bad eggs at any party."

The Donovan's house was massive; three stories with a glassed cupola atop the 3rd floor. Inside, the robot butler bowed to them, accepted the invitation Randal held out and handed them off to a robot footman who escorted them up the spiral staircase to the ballroom. The glass roof gave the impression the room was open to the night sky. Tash was interested to note although there was no formal receiving line, the footman checked them before announcing their names loudly enough to be heard over the music.

When they entered the ballroom, the guests were moving to the stately measures of the Pavane.

"I think we should have taken dance lessons," Devon whispered to Tash.

"Yes, I think you're right," she whispered back.

As the music ended, several couples came over to greet Judith and Randal and be introduced to the guests from earth. The newcomers from earth were welcomed by Randal and Judith's friends and soon enjoying themselves.

Tash soon found her fears about not knowing the dance steps were of no consequence. It was true she and Devon were unfamiliar with some of the steps used in the formal court dances, but the majority of those attending the party favored the livelier Country Dances. Watching Randal and Judith cavort in one of these dances, Tash realized, "Devon those are square dance steps!"

"What?" he asked.

"No, look at them. Remember back in our freshman year when we all had to learn the steps for that melodrama?"

He stared at the dancers for a moment. "You want to dance, don't you?"

"Yes," she admitted.

"Okay, when the next set forms we'll try it."

Randal was engaged in demonstrating a fencing move to Devon and several others. When a man Tash hadn't been introduced to asked her to dance, she accepted.

"My name is Jean Coudet," he said. He was tall and slim with delicately cut features. His looks didn't appeal to Tash, but she smiled and accepted the invitation.

It was a fast-moving line dance and when it was over, she found herself across the room from her friends.

She thanked Jean for the dance and headed back across the room.

"Hey, don't run off," he said.

"Sorry," she told him. "But I left my drink back on our table and I'm thirsty."

"Here," he said, "plucking a glass off a tray held by one of the robot servers. "Drink this. I'm sure it will do the trick."

The look was so quickly gone Tash thought she imagined the predatory gleam she saw in his eyes. She thanked him and took several swallows before she realized it tasted funny.

"What is this?" she asked. "It tastes funny."

"I'm sure it's fine," Jean said. "I bet you've never tasted Cocoa Berry juice before."

It had only been a few moments
since she swallowed the punch when
she commenced feeling dizzy and sick.
She pushed away from Jean, intending
to go and find Devon.

"Hey, don't rush away," he said,
grabbing her arm.

"I have to go. I'm sorry. I'm
sick," Tash gasped out. She tried to
pull away but his grip on her arm
tightened.

"Relax, you won't remember a
thing," he said.

"Jean, I don't know," one of the
others said. "She's turning green. I
think maybe she's about to barf."

"Grab her arm!" Jean snapped,
yanking on the laces at her waist.

Tash spotted Devon through a gap
in the crowd surrounding her and
yelled, "Devon! Help!"

"Shut up bitch!" Jean hissed.
"Filippo, put your hand over her
mouth to shut her up."

Before the tall dark man could obey him, Devon, Randal, and Judith came racing up. Devon jerked Jean around to face him and planted a fist in his face. Jean stumbled back and tripped over the man who had said Tash looked green. In the meantime, Randal delivered a New Orleans slap to the man who held Tash's other arm. The blow might have looked like a slap, but the actual strike was delivered with heel of the hand rather than the fingers. The man staggered, releasing her, and Judith put an arm around Tash to hold her steady.

Tash leaned over and threw up. She would have fallen if Judith hadn't been supporting her.

"What did you give her, you creep?" Judith glared at Jean over Tash's back. The girl from earth had sunk to her hands and knees, her body heaving with the force of the convulsions.

"I'm going to need some help,
here," Judith said. "I think she's
having a reaction to whatever they
gave her. We need to get her in to
have her stomach pumped."

Devon turned and pulled Tash to
her feet, sliding an arm under her
legs to carry her.

"I'll get the car," Randal said.
"Meet me out back," he told Judith.

Jean and the four others took
advantage of Devon and Randal's
preoccupation to slide away.

Their sled came gliding in as they
stepped out the back door onto the
backyard wharf. Devon sat with Tash
on his lap and the other two followed
him into the sled. Tash moaned,
turning her face into Devon's
shoulder. She had quit convulsing,
but her breathing was irregular.

"Med center. Fast!" Randal
ordered. "Tell them we're coming in
with a poison victim who might be
going into anaphylactic shock."

Judith dug out the sled's first aid kit and turned on the oxygen system. She put a mask over Tash's face and her breathing steadied.

The trauma team was waiting when their sled pulled into the Emergency unloading dock. The team put Tash on a gurney and started their own oxygen system.

"What did she take?" the doctor was young with tired looking eyes and trailed by a bevy of medical students.

"This isn't her fault!" Devon said, aggressively. "Someone slipped something into her drink at a party and she started convulsing and throwing up. You can't blame her for this!"

"Relax, tiger. I wasn't blaming her, but to treat it I do need to know what she took."

"I'm sorry, we're all a little on edge, Dr. Givens," Judith intervened, reading the man's name tag. "I think

it must have been a date-rape drug of
some kind. They were trying to get
her clothes off when we found them."

"Them? do you know who it was?"
Givens asked.

Judith exchanged a startled look
with Randal. "I saw Jean Coudet,
Sandro Malony, and Filippo
Bruenlleschi. Coudet and Malony both
had hold of her arms."

"Why does it matter?" Randal
asked.

"Because your friend isn't the
only victim who has been brought in
here with these symptoms this month."

He turned to the aide taking
notes. "It's probably Ribastar
Ultrivarix. Do a tox screen, and pump
her stomach, then prep an IV pressure
syringe with 1cc Halcitracin, after
five minutes, give her a mixed dose
of 1cc Halcitracin and Insuderal."

"What are you giving her?" Devon
asked.

"The Halcitracin is to counteract the Ribastar Ultrivarix and the Insuderal will counteract the allergic reaction."

"You can wait in the lounge until we have some news," one of the students told them, gesturing to a room off to the side.

After about an hour, Dr. Givens came to find them. "Your friend will be fine," he assured them. "In fact, you can take her home now if you want, but before you go, Officer Mendez wants to ask you some questions."

"I understand you saw the men who did this?" Officer Mendez was around forty, with the steady eyes and hands of a veteran cop.

"Yes, we did," Judith said. "I gave Dr. Givens their names."

Mendez nodded. "So," he said. Would you mind repeating it for my report?"

After they did so, Judith went to help Tash dress. Mendez eyed the two

young men grimly. "This is now a
police matter," he told them. "Don't
go hunting on your own, you hear?"

"Of course not," Randal said
innocently.

Mendez made a disgusted noise and
left.

"I don't think he believed you,"
Devon said.

They dropped the two girls off at
Randal's house, where his mother made
a fuss over Tash, and insisted she
lie down after her 'ordeal'.

Judith followed the two men out to
the door. "Randal Langton you be
careful!" she said. "You might fool
your mom and that cop, but I know
what you're going to do."

Randal laughed and brushed a kiss
across her mouth. "Careful is my
middle name," he said.

Judith glared after them. "I know
your middle name, and it isn't
careful!" she muttered to herself.

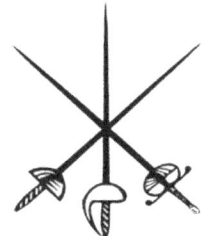

THE ARENA

"WHERE CAN WE find this guy?" Devon asked.

Randal considered a moment, before he called a friend of his. "Oliver where does Jean Coudet hang out?" he asked.

Oliver Coffyn looked back at him through the vid screen with a frown. He was a dark-skinned man with blue eyes and tight black curls. "Why do you want to know? He's nobody to mess around with."

"He tried to hurt a friend of mine tonight," Devon said. "He needs to be taught a lesson."

"A woman friend?" Oliver asked. "Who are you?"

"This is Devon Morton," Randal said. "He and Tash came back to Barsoom with me to work on a project."

"I've heard he can be found at the Golden Dragon," Oliver said. "I'll grab Ailwin and meet you there."

The Golden Dragon was well maintained outside; Avalon's city fathers would have demanded that. The elevated structure was made of Irregular shaped stones and hardwood beams. The stilts supporting the tavern were of stone as well. Unlike the Donovan's home, Devon saw no parking garage with robot driven sleds. Instead, the empty sleds seemed to be parked in a messy pattern around the building.

Oliver and another young man Randal introduced as Ailwin Doreward, a thin bespeckled man with sharp grey eyes, met them outside the tavern.

"I thought you might need backup,"
Oliver explained. "Coudet runs with
a pack."

"What do you intend to do?" Ailwin
asked Devon.

"Beat the crap out of him," Devon
said. "You have a problem with that?"

"No," Ailwin said, "but once the
first blow is struck, he'll probably
challenge you."

"So?"

"Do you intend to accept a
challenge?" Oliver asked.

"If I do, what does it mean?"
Devon asked.

"Then your seconds arrange a time
and place for the duel. As the one
challenged, the choice of weapons
will be yours. Are you any good with
a sword?"

"Does it have to be a sword? I'd
rather use a knife."

Ailwin's eyebrows rose. "It's been
done. Are you good?"

"I do okay," Devon said.

As they entered the tavern through the carved, hardwood door, Devon paused to take stock of the clientele. The tavern patrons were a rough looking bunch. Both men and women wore traditional renaissance dress of doublets and hose, but swords and other weapons were clearly on display.

Coudet and his posse were drinking at a back table. The crowd, sensing a confrontation, parted for Devon and his companions to approach them. Coudet and Sandro both still showed marks from the earlier confrontation.

"Stand up, Coudet," Devon said.

When the other man slowly rose and stepped out to meet him, Devon looked him over from his head to his heels.

"You ran away earlier Coudet. I guess you don't have the guts to take a man on in a fair fight," Devon sneered. "You drug girls so you can gang rape them. You're a coward."

An ugly murmur ran through the crowd at the accusation.

Coudet withdrew a glove from his belt and threw it in Devon's face. "Name your seconds," Coudet snarled.

Oliver handed Devon a glove from his own belt. "Throw it back at him," he said.

Devon remembered a scene from an old movie where the challenged party had to respond to being struck with a glove. He stepped forward and slapped Coudet with the glove before handing it back to Oliver.

"The three of us will act for him," Randal said. "Who will act for you?"

"Sandro, Luca and Filippo will act for me," Coudet said.

"As challenged, Devon, it's your choice of weapons," Randal said.

"Bowie knives," Devon said calmly.

Another murmur ran through the crowd. By choosing the deadly Bowie Knife rather than a customary poniard

or rapier, Davon had virtually announced the duel would not end at first blood.

Oliver had been reading his palm tab. "The Fields are clear this morning," he said, addressing Sandro. "Will that suit you?"

"We will be there," Sandro said.

Back at Randal's parent's house, his mother finally left the two girls alone.

"Try and get some sleep dear," Mrs. Langton, a plump motherly woman said, softly closing the door behind her.

Tash sat up in the bed. "Is she gone?" she whispered.

Judith nodded. "She means well," she said, keeping her voice low.

Tash opened her mouth, remembered in time the woman was going to be Judith's mother-in-law and asked instead, "What's bothering you? You're as tense as a bow string."

"I'm sure there's going to be a challenge over this," Judith said. "In fact, I think that's where Randal and Devon went; hunting for Jean Coudet."

"A challenge?" Tash repeated. "What's that?"

"It means a duel," Judith said grimly.

When Tash still looked puzzled, she said, "Randal didn't tell you much about life here, did he?"

"Well, we kind of avoid mentioning the colonies back in Laughing Mountain in case it gets back to the Portal Authority Agents."

"There is usually a lot of dueling among the younger men. It's how most arguments are settled here."

"You mean they fight each other?"

Judith nodded. "For simple things, it's usually ends with someone drawing first blood. For more serious things, like what happened to you— well, a duel can be deadly."

"What?" Tash exclaimed.

"Sssh! Keep your voice down," Judith said. "You didn't think Devon was going to ignore what happened to you, did you?"

"You think he is going to challenge this guy Coudet to fight?" Tash demanded.

"Yes, I do."

Tash swung her legs off the bed. "I have to stop him."

"Honey you can't do that," Judith said.

"Why not?" Tash demanded.

"If you do, the pair of you might as well go home," Judith said. "If he reneges on a challenge, he'll be branded a coward. No one will associate with him or do any kind of business with him. Is that what you want?"

Tash stared at her in shock. "But he could get killed!" she said.

Judith nodded. "Yes, I know. Is Devon any good with a sword?"

"I don't know," Tash said numbly.

Judith eyed her curiously. "*Could* you stop him?"

Tash slumped back on the bed. "Probably not. Back in high school there was this guy who started a rumor about me, and Devon got into a fight with him. When I told him I didn't want him fighting anyone on my behalf, he said it was none of my business. It was between him and his conscience. You said this dueling is a regular thing. Do you know where it's going to happen?"

"Why do you want to know?"

"I want to be there," Tash said. When Judith hesitated, she said, "I won't try to stop it, but I need to be there."

"Let me make a few calls," Judith said.

In Avalon, duels were held in Hyde Park. Designed after the famous one on Earth, it had bike and hiking trails, tall trees and other areas designed for enjoying the outdoors. The Dueling Fields were separated from the rest of the park by a hedge of tall boxwood bushes surrounding them. Behind the hedge was a secondary wall to absorb projectiles. A second hedge hid the wall from the recreational areas of the park. The dueling field was a grassy area about fifty feet around and graded to make it smooth. Spectators were allowed if they stayed behind the fenced off area. Once the field had been booked by the seconds an audience usually came to watch. Most duels were conducted with bladed weapons, but on the rare occasion, if pistols were chosen, the secondary wall behind the hedge would absorb the impact.

A row of sleds was parked along the edge of the green behind the area marked for spectators. One of them bore the tell-tale red cross of an ambulance. Judith parked her sled

along the edge practically under the
boxwoods.

When Tash unbuckled her seat belt,
she said, "Stay in the car. We'll
watch on the long-range traffic cam."

She turned on the monitor and cued
it in for a closeup of the men
standing near the center of the
field.

As they watched, Devon lifted one
of the huge knives and walked himself
through a knife drill to wake up his
memory muscle. Finally, he pulled a
strand of hair out and tested the
knife's sharpness by slashing through
it.

Devon had changed out of his
frilly shirt and Doublet. Instead, he
wore a sleeveless leather vest and
tight leather pants. Tash stared. It
had been years since she had seen
Devon stripped for fighting. She
remembered his body as soft and a
little doughy. Nothing could be
further from the truth today. He now

had a tight abdomen and heavily muscled shoulders and arms from extensive work in the gym and in the Mixed Martial Arts Arena sponsored by the Blue Moon Militia. The leather pants molded to the muscles in his thighs and calves.

Judith noticed her stare and grinned. "See something you like?" she inquired with a smile.

"That can't be Devon," Tash said. "Where did he get all those muscles?"

"Maybe you haven't been looking," Judith said.

"I haven't seen him fight since we were teenagers," Tash admitted. "The Militia doesn't encourage spectators at their training drills."

"He's a member of this Militia?" Juliette asked curiously.

Tash made a face. "Almost every teenage boy joins, and even some of the girls. Not my thing though, so I didn't."

She turned back to the monitor. "Who is that?"

Judith turned on the vid mic so they could hear what was being said.

A tall spare man with hard eyes came forward. Randal and the other seconds went to meet him.

"I am Robierre Le Grande. I will be officiating at this duel. Are both parties here?"

"My principal is here," Randal said.

"So is mine," Sandro replied.

"Is there a doctor present?"

"Dr. Givens from the Emergency clinic," Givens announced.

"You get around," Randal told him.

Robierre looked at them with a frown. "Do you know each other?"

"We met for the first time tonight in the ER when Mr. Langeton and his principal brought in a young lady who had been poisoned by a date rape drug," Givens answered.

"And the weapons?"

Randal opened the case he had been carrying and held it out. "Here are my principal's weapons of choice, your honor."

Robierre turned to Sandro. "You have inspected the weapons and are satisfied with them?"

"Yes," Sandro said.

He turned to Randal, "And you?"

"If you don't mind?" Devon intervened. "I'm more familiar with this type of weapon."

The judge nodded. "Very well."

Devon picked up one of the knives, balancing it in his hand. He held the tip to his eyes, scrutinizing it carefully. "The point looks sharp enough," he said. He pulled out a piece of paper and made a quick, slashing move with the tip end of the blade. When it sliced cleanly through, he nodded.

"This one is fine," he said. He repeated the same actions with the second knife, before replacing it in the box. "This one is fine as well."

"Very well," Robierre said. "Gentlemen, choose your weapons."

When the judge's assistant held out the box to Randal, he gestured to Sandro. "Please. We want no questions about the legitimacy of the duel."

Scowling, Sandro grabbed one of the knives and held it out to Coudet.

Devon accepted his and did another quick knife drill.

Robierre gestured for them to come to the center of the field.

It was apparent Coudet had been taught the rudiments; his stance was correct, one leg slightly behind the other, with the knife in a loose forty-five angle. He was studying Devon thoughtfully, almost as if he was waiting for something.

When Devon grinned at him, he blinked and glanced at Brunelleschi with a quick jerk of his head.

Brunelleschi nodded and disappeared into the crowd.

Devon took his own stance, holding his knife as he had been taught; arm at ninety degrees with the knife held at a forty-five-degree angle and his free hand above it, guarding his throat.

Out of the corner of his eye, he saw the judge drop his handkerchief and immediately took several quick, short bouncing steps forward, at the same time slashing downward with his knife at Coudet's fingers, then a reverse upward slash.

Coudet jerked his hand back involuntarily when Devon's knife opened a shallow cut. Unfortunately, the blow hadn't been deep enough to slice the tendons. A flash of light hit Devon's peripheral vision and he heard a scuffle in the watching crowd. He ignored both things, concentrating on Coudet.

Angrily, Coudet slashed back,
missing because Devon had pivoted to
his ten o'clock, following it with
another slash, this time at the
inside of Coudet's front leg.
Coudet's padded pants protected his
femoral artery, but the cut opened a
bloody gash on the inside of his
thigh.

Not giving his opponent time to
recover, Devon feinted at Coudet's
eyes, before stabbing him in the
neck, using a combination of the
stab/slash sequence he had been
taught.

Blood spurted back at Devon,
narrowly missing blinding him, and
the few seconds it took for him to
dodge, gave Coudet the time to stab
at Devon's back. Coudet's knife angle
was off though, and instead of a
clean stab, the knife slid down,
opening a cut at Devon's waist before
getting tangled in his waistband.

Devon grabbed Coudet's knife hand and did another combination slash and stab at his leg, following it with one to his knife hand. This time Coudet stumbled, and his knees hit the ground, dropping the knife. Devon held the man's knife arm up, exposing the brachial artery.

"Do you yield?" he asked.

Almost unconscious from pain, Coudet nodded. "I yield."

Devon dropped his opponent and stepped back, gesturing for the doctor.

"You are declared the winner. I decree honor has been satisfied," Robierre stated.

Coffyn and Ailwin man-handled Brunelleschi forward. "A moment, Your Honor," Ailwin said. "There is a small matter of attempted interference in the duel by one of Coudet's seconds."

Coffyn held out Brunelleschi's
hand and forced it open. A small hand
mirror fell out.

"He used this to try and blind
Devon during the fight," Ailwin said.

"My girlfriend dropped it, and I
picked it up for her," Brunelleschi
protested. "Flashing it at the
duelists wasn't intentional."

"Where is this young lady?"
Robierre asked.

"I'm here, Your Honor." A short,
slightly plump woman in her early
twenties came forward.

"Is what he says true?" Robierre
asked.

"Yes, I thought I had a spot on my
face, and I dropped my mirror. I'm
sorry Your Honor," she said.

The judge looked at them
consideringly before he nodded. He
knew he could check the veracity of
the girl's statement on the cameras
broadcasting the duel, but it was
late, and this was his third duel

this evening, "You can let him go. In the future, young lady I suggest you not attempt to repair your makeup during a duel. If it turns out the broadcast vids don't agree with your story, further steps may be taken," he warned.

Once the duel was finished, Judith hadn't been able to keep Tash in the vehicle.

"Devon Morton, don't you dare do this again! Do you hear me?" Tash shouted, coming to a sliding halt in front of him. She hit him in the shoulder with her fist. "You could have been killed—"

Devon was still riding the adrenalin high from the fight. He yanked the angry Tash into his arms, fastening his mouth fiercely on hers.

Tash was fighting a similar rush of adrenalin. Heart pounding, she melted against him, her body trying to mold itself into his.

Oliver coughed. "No wish to interrupt, but Dr. Givens wants to look at the wound on your back Devon."

Devon lifted his head and stepped back. Tash's arms slid from around his neck. She was staring at him as if she had never seen him before.

"So now you know," he said.

Tash lifted trembling fingers to her mouth.

"Pull off your vest," Givens ordered, pulling out a disinfectant spray.

Judith put an arm around Tash and turned her toward the parked sleds. "Come on, Hon, let's get you home," she said.

MURDER & MAYHEM

SIMONE GUSSET parked her sled under the trees at the edge of the garage slots attached to Dreamedia Laboratory, the facility owned by Timothy Langeton and his two partners. When she stepped out of her sled, she stood a long time scanning the area around the lab before she was sure no one was around. It was after midnight and she suspected her boss in the Red Conclave was having her watched, but she had been careful to make sure she lost the tail before she came here. She had dressed to blend into the night; a dark, mottled skinsuit clung to her excellent figure. She had added a dark helmet with a night vision visor. She worked

here during the day, but she didn't
want anyone to realize she was making
an unauthorized visit tonight.

Dr. Langeton and his partners thought
none of the lab techs realized Randal
had returned from earth with a valuable
data crystal. Her first week working at
Dreamedia Labs, Simone had planted
listening devices in all the partners'
offices and in the lab where they
commonly worked together so she knew
everything going on. As instructed, she
had reported the find to her boss in Red
Conclave, and he had ordered her to steal
it. She intended to obey of course, it
would be worth her life not to, but she
also intended to make a copy of the data
crystal. Simone was an opportunist. If
she could copy the information, she
figured she could sell it for enough to
set her up for life.

When the lab closed for the evening,
Dr. Langeton had locked the crystal
inside the vault. Privately, Simone
thought the word 'secure' for a room she
had managed to obtain the codes for her
first week was laughable.

It took her only a few minutes to open the lab door and shut off the security vids. The vault where they had secured the crystal was as easy to open. She took an empty crystal out of her pocket and set the office copy machine to transfer a copy of the data.

Not wanting to take the copy with her in case her boss had her searched, she hid the copy in the base of one of the flowering plants Mrs. Langeton had used to decorate the office. Simone had barely closed the Security door when a voice spoke behind her.

"I'll take that," he said.

She turned around to face Antoni Giuseppe, her boss's right hand operative. Giuseppe was a small, non-descript man whose specialty was hiding in plain sight. He was also a stone killer.

"No," she said. "I was told to bring it to him myself."

"Not going to happen, girlie," he said. "He's decided he can't trust you. Did you think he wouldn't find out about your little blackmail schemes?"

"What schemes?" she demanded, her heart in her throat. "I haven't been blackmailing anybody he doesn't know about."

"Oh, please," Giuseppe said. "He knows you went to all the partners and demanded money not to tell their wives you were sleeping with them. You didn't turn it in, Girlie."

"Underhill is the only one who agreed to pay me. He hasn't paid it yet," she said. "I'm going to turn it in as soon as he does."

Giuseppe took out a poniard and flipped it from hand to hand. "You're a fool," he said.

Simone watched the knife the way a small animal watched a viper as it prepared to strike.

"You can't kill me here," she said. "They have inside security vids. You'll show on them."

"But you so kindly turned them off," he said. The knife throw was fast and sure. The poniard buried itself hilt deep into her heart.

"No!" she cried and tried to run, her hands pressing the knife to her chest. She staggered and fell a few inches from where she had been standing.

Giuseppe watched her die before he removed the knife, wiping it on her clothes before he slid it into the sheath under his sleeve. He searched her pockets until he found the crystal. He put it in his own pocket before leaving.

Once outside, he set the alarm to go off in twenty minutes before mounting his air sled and speeding away.

The policeman who responded to the shrilling alarm found the front door open. He went inside and discovered Simone's body.

Shaking his head at the waste of such a pretty woman, he called in the homicide and waited for the coroner and detectives to arrive.

MY FEET UPON THE MOONLIT DUST

TASH WAS barely regaining her equilibrium when they arrived back at Randal's house and found a police sled parked in front.

"Judith, isn't that a police sled?" Tash asked.

"Yes, it is. I wonder what they're doing here."

"They haven't come looking for Devon and Randal for the duel, have they?"

"Don't be silly. Dueling is legal. They wouldn't be here for that," Judith replied as they alit from the carriage.

"There is someone sitting in the back," Tash said. "On earth, the person in the back seat is usually being arrested."

"That can't be right. That's my father," Judith said.

Even as she spoke, two policemen came out of the residence with a man in handcuffs.

"Isn't that Randal's father?" Tash asked.

"Yes. I'm going to find out what's going on." Judith dashed over to the sled. "What are you doing?" she asked.

"Papa Timothy, what's going on?"

"Stay back, Miss," the policeman closest to her blocked her path.

"Please go in the house Judith," the man already in the sled spoke.

"Daddy?" she said. "What's going on?"

"Allison will explain everything. Please go inside girls," Randal's father said.

Judith watched numbly as Randal's father was also put in the sled and driven away.

Now it was Tash who put an arm around Judith. "Let's go on in," she said. "Surely Mrs. Langeton knows what has happened."

Allison Langeton had collapsed on a sofa, weeping bitterly. Judith immediately went to her. When she touched the older woman's shoulder, Allison turned to her sobbing. "They've taken him! They took my husband."

"But why?" Judith asked.

"If you can get her calm enough to answer some questions, it will go better for her and her husband," A woman said.

"Who are you?" Judith demanded.

"I'm Detective Serena Addicock, and this is Detective Johan Straus," the woman said. She was in her early thirties, with dishwater blond hair, cut in a short bob. She had a trim athletic body.

Tash went to the kitchen and asked the robot server to bring a glass of water for Mrs. Langeton.

"I want to know why you are here," Judith said. "I want to know why you've arrested Professor Langeton and my father."

"Perhaps it would be better if we all introduced ourselves," Detective Straus said. He was in his forties, with a long, narrow face and dark brown hair pulled back in a long tail. "May I have your names please?"

Tash took the glass of water from the server and held it out to Randal's mother. "Try a little water, Mrs. Langeton."

Randal's mother took the glass in a shaking hand and tried to drink it. Judith caught it before she could drop it and held it to her lips.

"Thank you," she whispered.

"My name is Tash Higgins. I'm visiting here from earth," Tash said. "This is Judith Garneys, Randal Langeton's fiancée."

"And where is Mr. Langeton now?"

"I'm right here. Who the hell are
you?" Randal demanded as he and Devon
entered the room.

Judith thrust the glass into Tash's
hand and ran to him. "Randal, they've
arrested our fathers! They won't tell me
why—"

"Alright," he said, putting an arm
around her. Before he could say anything
else, his mother jumped up and flung
herself at him. Randal received her in
his other arm, patting her on the back.

"Okay, Mom," he said, soothingly.
"Let me find out what is going on, okay?
You and Judith wait in the parlor."

Gently he handed his mother off to
Judith, who put an arm around her and
led her into the next room. Tash
hesitated before following them.

Once inside, she left the door partly
open so she and Judith could hear what
wat was going forward.

Judith settled her prospective
mother-in-law on the setee, handing her
the glass of water. Mrs. Langeton sipped
it, occasionally giving a gulping sob.

"Can you tell us where you've been this evening, Mr. Langeton?" Detective Straus asked.

"Certainly, I can tell you, providing *you* tell *me* what is going on here." Randal said.

"A woman was killed at Dreamedia Laboratory tonight. We naturally need to know where everyone connected to the lab was tonight."

"Devon and I were at the dueling fields earlier," Randal said. "Before, we were at Mercy Hospital Emergency Room."

"Why were you at those places?"

"We were at a party, and someone slipped Tash a date rape drug in her drink. She had an allergic reaction to it," Devon said.

"And you've been together the entire evening?" Detective Addicock asked.

"Yes," Randal said. "Where is my father?"

"All three partners have been detained as material witnesses in the murder," Straus replied. "Unfortunately, your mother became incoherent when asked her whereabouts this evening. If you can get her to answer that, we'll be on our way."

"Why have my father and Professor Garneys been detained?"

"I'm afraid we can't discuss an ongoing investigation with you."

"I see. I should tell you my mother is obviously too upset to speak further with you tonight. I assume she has been in all evening. You have my permission to check it with the server bots. You may speak further to her tomorrow when she has the support of the family lawyer."

Straus looked at him thoughtfully. Randal met his eyes, his own hard. Straus nodded, recognizing when he had hit a wall. "Very well, if you'll direct me to the robot controller room, my partner and I can be on our way. Please inform your mother we would like her to come to the station house tomorrow to make a statement. She can, of course bring a lawyer."

Randal watched them leave, frowning, before he went to the house vid screen

and tapped into it. "Agustino DaVinci," he ordered.

"Records indicate Signore DaVinci will have left the office by this time," the server reported.

"Com him at home, then," Randal said.

DaVinci had obviously been asleep when he came to the vid screen. "You aren't Timothy Langeton," he said.

"I'm his son Randal. My father has been detained as a material witness in a murder case. So has Professor Garneys. I would appreciate it if you could try and get bail for them. Also, detectives investigating the case want to see mother at the 12th precinct tomorrow. Could someone from your office be there to represent her?"

"Of course," DaVinci said. "Are you being detained as well?"

"I have an alibi," Randal told him. "I was at the dueling grounds during the time in question."

"I see. Please tell your mother I'll meet her at the Police Station tomorrow. Remind her not to say anything unless I okay it."

"I will." Randal signed off.

"Sorry about this," he told Devon.

"Hey, this isn't your fault," Devon said.

In the parlor, Tash was saying the same sort of thing to Judith.

"Do you need to com your mom and let her know what's going on?" Tash asked her.

"I guess I'd better," Judith said. She looked anxiously at Mrs. Langeton. "Will you be okay with her?"

"Yes, you com your mom."

Tamara Garneys wasn't hysterical, but she wasn't calm either.

"Did you call Ava?" Judith asked her.

"She can't get here until tomorrow," Tamara told her. "Did they arrest Timothy too?"

"Yes," Judith said. "Allison's pretty upset. Why don't you join us here? The two of you can keep each other company. I'll send the carriage for you."

"Judith's dad should probably have a rep with him too," Devon said when Randal got off the com with the lawyer.

"You're right, but I don't know who it is," he said.

"I bet Judith does."

"Yeah,"

Devon saw him brace himself before going into the room where his mother and the girls waited.

Everything seemed much calmer.

Judith looked up when they came in. "Are they gone."

"Yes. Judith do th you have a family lawyer?"

"I think it's Carlos Santana. Why?"

" I sent ours to go and be with Dad at the precinct. Your dad should have a rep with him too."

"Oh, thank you, Randal. I didn't think of that. I think I have his com address." She fumbled with her com. "Here it is. I sent it to you."

He nodded and he and Devon left the room.

"He's a good man," Tash said.

"I know," Judith said ruefully. "But I wish he cared about me the way Devon feels about you."

"What makes you think he doesn't?"

"Three letters in six months? And he never once said he missed me. I've never gotten the kind of kiss Devon gave you after the duel either."

"For a first kiss it was quite something," Tash admitted. "But I keep wondering how much of it was real and how much was adrenaline."

"Oh, there was a lot of adrenaline," Judith agreed, "but it was real alright."

The ornate door knocker sounded, and they heard the robo server say, "Welcome Mrs. Garneys."

"We're in here, Mom," Judith called.

Mrs. Garneys was a petite blond, whose hair was beginning to show silver. "Is that tea?" She asked. "I'd love a cup."

"I'll tell the server," Tash said.

Judith looked anxiously at her mother. "Randal called Carlos Santana to go to the precinct to be with Dad."

Tamara nodded. "Yes, he told me when I came in. Do you know why they've been detained?"

"No, we don't. Do you?"

"That horrible Simone Gusset woman broke into the lab tonight and someone killed her. The police must have found copies of those blackmail letters she sent your father in her comp."

"The one's threatening to tell you Dad was sleeping with her? But those were months ago. Besides he told her to tell and be damned. I still don't understand why he didn't fire her."

"I don't either, but it had something to do with why they hired her in the first place. One of those government agencies wanted her watched I think."

"Why didn't Dad tell the Detectives that?"

Her mother made a disgusted noise.
"Apparently, they all took an oath of
secrecy. Well, I didn't, and I'll say
so if they don't let your father go!"

"Timothy got one of those letters
as well," Allison said. "He showed it
to me."

"That detective said all of the
partners had been detained," Judith
said. "Gamel isn't married. I wonder
who Simone threatened to tell?"

"He gambles," Tamara said. "Maybe
she threatened to tell someone about
his I.O.Us."

"Is he badly in debt?" Tash asked.
"As long as he pays them off, there
wouldn't be anything to blackmail him
about."

"It's worth looking into," Judith
said.

TRIALS & TRIBULATIONS

"AFTER I arranged a bail hearing for your father in the morning," Agustino DaVinci told Randal. "A man caught me as I left the Precinct. He threatened to harm me and my family if I didn't drop your father as a client."

"What? Who was it?"

DaVinci shrugged. "He didn't give his name, He was a little, dark man with no distinguishing features."

"What are you going to do?"

DaVinci's smile was feral. "It's not the first time someone has tried to intimidate me. I have an excellent bodyguard service I use when this happens. I thought you might want to know about the threat, so you can take your own precautions."

"Did you report the threat to the investigating officers?"

"Yes. Not sure they believed me."

"Thank you for telling me." Randal got off the com with a frown.

"Trouble?" Devon asked.

"Maybe," he said slowly. "Dad's lawyer told me he and his family were threatened. Someone wants him to drop Dad as a client."

Devon's eyebrows rose. "Think he'll do that?"

"No, in fact, he seemed kind of perked about it. Said he has a bodyguard service he uses in cases like this."

"It sounds to me as if someone wants your dad and his partners to take the fall for the murder."

"I think he's right," Judith said. "We put your mom and mine to bed. I gave your mom a sleeping pill."

"Thanks," Randal said. "How is your mom taking it?"

"She's okay," Judith said. "Mostly she's mad. Kept talking about how Dad and the others were asked to employee Simone because some hush-hush agency wanted to keep an eye on her."

"Why did she go to the lab tonight?" Tash asked. "I mean, what made tonight special enough to break into the offices?"

Randal and Devon exchanged looks. "The data crystal," they said together.

"Can we check to see if it's there?" Devon asked.

"Let's go find out," Randal said. "You girls don't let anybody in while we're gone. If they threatened DaVinci, it's possible they might come here."

"Does the house have a security lockdown mode?" Tash asked.

"Yes," Randal said. He went to the vid console and keyed in a sequence. "There, I've put it in secure mode."

The vid screen divided itself into sections, each one showing an approach to the house.

"The robo servers have also activated the security mode," he said. "Let them screen any coms and answer the doors, okay."

"Okay," Judith said. "Umm, I hate to ask this, but Licorice needs a sandbox or something."

"Tell the servers, I'm sure they'll find something he can use."

Randal went to the wall cabinet and pressed a panel. He took out two pulse pistols, offering one to Devon, who strapped it on. He also handed the earthman a seven-inch knife in a sheath, selecting a rapier for himself.

"We've got air sleds in the garage," he said.

Tash and Judith watched the two men leave. Neither one had any intention of sleeping until they returned.

"I don't know about you," Tash said, "But I could do with a glass of wine."

"That's an excellent idea," Judith said.

When Devon and Randal arrived at Dreamedia Laboratories, only one police sled was still parked in front and the front door had a Police Seal.

"They've sealed the building," Devon said.

"Only the front door," Randal replied. He dismounted his sled and led the way to a side door. He entered a code and it slid open.

The vault appeared to be closed, but when they examined it, Devon said, "This has been opened sometime around midnight."

Grimly, Randal keyed in the code and the heavy steel door slid to one

side. The drawer holding the crystal
was open and empty. "It's gone,"
Randal said.

"Freeze!" an authoritive voice
said.

Devon raised his hands and turned
around. The man who had ordered them
to freeze wore a policeman's uniform.
He was also holding a pulse pistol
aimed at them.

"My name is Randal Langeton, and
I have every right to be here,"
Randal told him.

"Show me your ID," the man said.

Randal reached inside his jacket
and pulled out a badge. He held it so
the cop could see it.

"What's that?" he demanded.

"Run a scanner over it," Randal
said.

Frowning, the man took out a
portable scanner and aimed it at the
badge. A blue light ran over it. He
nearly dropped the scanner when a
voice came out of the badge.

"Authorization level Blue. Bearer has authorized Clearance in all security matters. Cooperation is required."

"What the Hell?"

"An important piece of technology is missing. We need to know if it was taken into evidence."

"I don't have an evidence list. The detectives probably have one."

"Then contact them. Now."

"They've probably gone off duty by now," He protested.

"Do you like your job?" Randal asked him.

"I'm a good cop, mister," was the reply.

"Then com the detectives."

"Okay, okay, don't get your—never mind."

Devon looked thoughtfully at his friend, nodding to himself, as he realized he had been correct about why Randal had been chosen to come to earth to plant the protection virus into the Portal Authority programming.

He crossed his arms, half-sitting on a nearby desk. It shifted a little and he grabbed the edge, accidentally brushing the fronds of the large plant next to it. His eye caught a flash of light when the frond moved. He bent down and brushed at the potting soil. When he did, he found the hard surface of a crystal. His fingers closed around it, and he examined it. He held it out so Randal could see it. Randal nodded and pantomimed putting in a pocket. Devon did so.

The cop had his back to them while he spoke to the detective he had gotten out of bed.

"I know," he was explaining, "but this guy has high-level authority. What level? I think that badge thing said Blue Level. He says an important piece of tech is missing and he wants to know if we've got it in evidence."

"Give me a minute. I'll com the evidence lockup and ask them to check. What does this tech look like?"

"She wants to know what to look for," the officer said, turning around.

"It's a data crystal," Randal told him.

"Did you get that?"

"I got it. I'll com you back."

A few minutes later, Addicock commed back. "No, we didn't find anything like that. How important is it?"

"Very important," Randal told her. "I would bet it's what Gusset broke in here to steal."

"Who had access to it?"

"All three partners had access. They had no reason to steal it. I'm thinking Gusset's partner killed her for it."

"We didn't find any evidence of a partner."

"No," Randal agreed, "you were too busy pulling outdated blackmail letters off her computer. I suggest you look deeper into her criminal connections."

"How do you know she had criminal connections?"

"That's classified. You don't have clearance. Take my word for it—she had criminal connections."

"Dammit—" Addicock said.

"Goodnight, Detective," Randal said. "C'mon Devon. Let's go back to the house."

THIS WAY WE WERE LED

Judith studied her family lawyer, wondering how good an attorney he was. Carlos Santana had the quintessential Latin hero vibe perfect. He was tall and slender, with finely cut features. His dark hair had a touch of grey. He boasted an olive complexion and melting dark eyes with absurdly long lashes.

"I thought it would be better if I escorted the two of you to the police station to make your statements," he said.

"Do you think those detectives suspect Dad killed her?" She asked.

He smiled reassuringly at her. "What they think doesn't matter. It's what they can prove that counts."

"Oh," she said. She looked up in relief when Randal came into the room.
"Randal, this our family lawyer, Carlos Santana. This is my fiancée, Randal Langeton."

"Pleased to meet you," Randal said. "Did you come to escort Tamara to the police station?"

"Yes, and Miss Garneys as well."
"I had hoped Judith would ride in with me. My mother depends on her for support during this difficult time."

"And her own mother doesn't?"

"My mother is a tough lady," Judith said. "Besides, Ava arrived this morning, and— "

"I'll be accompanying our mother." The woman who spoke was several years older than Judith, taller and Her hair wasn't quite so bright a shade of red. "I'm Ava," she said, coming forward to shake his hand.

"Please call me Carlos," he said, retaining his grip on her hand a little longer than necessary. "Your mother is fortunate to have two such strong and lovely daughters."

Ava flushed a little under his admiring gaze. "Thank you."

Since Devon wanted to look over the copied crystal's programming, he and Tash had agreed to stay behind.

Judith handed Licorice to Tash. "I don't want to take him down there," she said. "Do you mind?"

Of course not," Tash told her, cuddling the small animal who sniffed her ear and whuffled.

Like most of Barsoom's buildings, the Police station floated on a slab anchored to Savano's lakebed. The station itself was three stories tall with eight sides. Next door, an octagon-shaped, 3 story open lattice structure held vehicles of all kinds, both official and private.

Randal parked in a visitor's parking area, and he and Judith got out. DaVinci met them at the entrance.

When they entered, they found Santana, Tamara, and Ava already waiting at the desk.

Inside the precinct house, plastic computer consoles sat on clear acrylic desks. Detectives in casual clothing and uniformed Patrolmen sat, stood, and performed various tasks. The clear, thick acrylic partitions muted the noise level. Along the far wall were holding cells, some empty, some full.

Straus and Addicock walked up as the officer manning the front desk was directing them to a waiting room.

"Good morning," Detective Addicock said.

Eyeing the detective, Judith felt frumpy. Despite being awake most of

the night, the woman looked fresh and crisp.

"Good morning, Detective," Randal said. "As requested, we are all here."

"So, I see," Addicock replied. "Mrs. Langeton, we'll take you first. This way please."

Smiling reassuringly at Randal's mother, DaVinci took her elbow and the two of them followed the detective into an interrogation room.

"Mrs. Garney's, if you will follow me, we'll try to get you out of here as soon as we can," Straus said.

Judith, Randal, and Ava followed the desk officer into the waiting room.

"There's coffee, if you want some," he said. "I can't swear how fresh it is, but it's hot."

"Thank you," Ava told him. "But we're good."

As soon as he departed, Ava turned to Randal and her sister. "Why did they arrest Dad?" she demanded.

Randal shrugged. "They think both your father and mine had motives to kill her."

"Why?" Ava repeated.

"They found some old e-mails from her threatening to tell their wives she was sleeping with them," Judith said in disgust. "They were over five months old."

"Did they find records of payments to her?"

"They aren't sharing," Randal told her. "I'm pretty sure they both told her to go to Hell. My mother knew about the threats. So did yours."

"Something else you should know; DaVinci was threatened in an attempt to get him to drop Dad as a client."

"Is he going to?" Ava asked.

Randal grinned. "Nope, he seems to be looking forward to a good fight."

"I wonder if Carlos was threatened as well," Ava said slowly.

"And maybe the investigating officers?" Judith put in.

"It's possible. In any event, I plan to do some poking around on my own," Randal said.

"I'm going with you," Judith declared.

"Ah—I thought Devon and I would go," Randal said.

"You do what you want," Judith retorted. "Simone's roommate is a woman, she might talk to me easier than to you. I'll take Tash with me when I go to see her."

Randal eyed her with frustration. In view of the threat DaVinci had received, Randal would have preferred she and the other women remain secure in the house. However, he could see from the obstinate set of her jaw Judith had no intention of agreeing to stay safely tucked away.

THE BLACK TEMPLARS

ACROSS TOWN in a small café, three men and two women were enjoying a cup of coffee. The Black Templars had been created back on earth, when the group was organizing to create an illegal colony. The group's original purpose was to keep an eye out for anyone attempting to betray their existence to Earth-Gov's Portal Authority. Now days, although still watching for any attempts to betray the existence of the colony to Earth-Gov, they had widened their scope of activities to include investigating the criminal activities plaguing Barsoom, the most pernicious of which was the Red Conclave. The Templars had only minimal official standing, but they had members everywhere, some active and some not, but their tentacles reached into all kinds of legal and illegal groups.

Andri Gauvreau was in his eighth decade, but his sharp blue eyes still held the intelligence he was famous for. "Simone Gusset was killed last night," he said.

"How did it happen?" Mathieu Heroux asked. Heroux was nearing fifty. Officially he was retired from his job on the actual ruling council.

"Stabbed to death," Joan Merton answered. Joan was a trim sixty and still beautiful, due to her excellent bone structure.

"How much did our agents learn about her activities?" Thomasine Villers asked. Thomasine was in her thirties, with bright blond hair. Her official profession was journalism, but she kept her hand in Templar activities.

"Unfortunately, the police arrested them for her murder," Guillaume Peele said. Unlike Villers, Peele was a famous theater actor and starred in many vids. He shook his handsome head in dismay.

"It's going to cause a lot of problems. I received a com message from Garney's wife. Apparently, he told her more about us than he was allowed to. She knows we asked Dreamedia Labs to hire Simone and to keep her on after she tried her little blackmail scheme on the two partners."

"Ouch," Villers said. "What else did she say?"

"She had a lot to say, but the gist of it was either we clear her husband and his partners of this crime, or she will go to the press with the entire story."

Gauvreau shrugged. "Our operative Randal Langeton is back from earth. He is already investigating. I think we can leave the matter in his hands."

"He's good at what he does," Merton admitted. "He managed to not only get the virus preventing Earth-Gov and the Portal Authority from finding our colony inserted into the PA's search program, but he also brought back a program for finding new worlds; I understand it also has the codes for reaching out to the other Outlawed Colonies."

"Yes, and he made a valuable contact. Devon Morton, the man who accompanied him back to Barsoom, is the acknowledged Portal expert for all the colonies," Peele said.

"I don't know," Heroux said. "That Morton might be a troublemaker; he's been here less than a day and already he's fought a duel."

Gauvreau laughed. "My old friend Robierre officiated at that duel. He tells me Morton opted for Bowie knives instead of swords or pistols."

"Most earthers don't have our skill. Did Coudet hurt him?"

"No, apparently it was Coudet who was overmatched; Robierre said Morton could have killed Coudet at any time during the duel. In fact, when he offered Coudet the option of surrender, Morton was in a position to kill him, and apparently he was willing to do so."

"I've heard some nasty rumors about Coudet and his crew," Villers said.

"What kind of rumors?"

"It seems a number of our young ladies have gone missing while attending a party. Afterwards they are brought into the emergency room. Medical staff says they show evidence they've been drugged, and gang raped. According to the police who interviewed them, they were last seen in Coudet's company."

"Perhaps we should look into this more closely," Peele said. "It might tie in with the rumors I've heard about a new drug going around."

THE ROOMMATE

JEANNINE SILVERTON, Simone's roommate was about five ten and model thin. When they commed her to say they wanted to talk about Simone, she hadn't been exactly welcoming, but after a moment, she had agreed. When they arrived, she looked the two girls over as if she smelled something bad. "Well, aren't you just the cutest thing," she said to Judith, with a saccharine smile.

If Jeannine had expected to intimidate the much smaller Judith, she had mistaken her woman. Judith's small stature occasionally led others to think she was as delicate as she was tiny, but

as Tash had discovered over the last few
days, Judith was about as easy to
intimidate as a bag of Cement.

"Why, thank you," Judith said as
sweetly. "I'm sorry to bother you when I
can see you aren't feeling well. Have
you seen a doctor?"

"A doctor? For what? I feel fine."

"Oh, dear, I shouldn't have mentioned
the weight loss—sometimes people with
your condition are so sensitive. I do
apologize."

Jeannine stared at her a moment,
before her mouth stretched into a
reluctant grin. "Okay," she said.
"Points even. You aren't at all the way
Simone described you."

Judith grinned back at her. "Pax?"

Jeannine laughed. "Pax," she agreed.
"Won't you sit down?"

"Thanks. This is Tash Higgens; she's
just arrived from earth."

Once Jeannine started talking, it
would have been impossible to stop her.
Neither Tash nor Judith tried.

"We're sorry your roommate was killed," Tash said. "Do you know of anyone who might want to hurt her?"

"Just about anybody who knew her, I imagine," Jeannine said. "We're cousins. We started rooming together in college and stayed roommates because neither of us could afford to move out. If I could, I would have."

"Oh, wow," Tash said sympathetically. "What are you going to do now?"

Jeannine grimaced. "Advertise for another roommate, I guess."

"Do you know what Simone was into lately?" Judith asked.

"I tried not to find out," Jeannine said frankly. "She liked to collect dirt on everyone. Sometimes she'd ask for money not to say what she knew, sometimes for other favors."

"What happened when her victims wouldn't cooperate?"

"She got back at them some way. I know she sent anonymous tips to the police hot-lines a couple of times, and I think she caused several divorces."

"Anyone recently?"

"You mean besides your father?"
Jeannine asked.

"He told her no, and he told my mom
about it," Judith said.

Jeannine laughed. "I heard. She was
pretty mad about that. She told me
Langeton was the better looking of the
trio who own the lab, but he wasn't
having any either. She would have liked
a chance at the son, but he was off
planet when she started working there."

"Wasn't she afraid you might turn on
her?" Tash asked.

Jeannine shook her head. "She and I
were about even on secrets because of
some stuff we did when we were kids."

"The thing with my father happened
over four months ago. Did she have any
recent victims?"

Jeannine sat still, thoughtfully
running a stylus through her fingers.
"Maybe. If I were you, I'd check to see
if any money is missing from the lab.
That's another thing she was into. She'd
get a job someplace, stay long enough to
figure out how the finances worked and
then do a little embezzling."

At Judith's look of surprise, she added, "Simone had a degree in business accounting."

"The missing money would turn up sooner or later. How did she keep from being found out?"

"Simone made some connections with a man who washed the money for her. I think he also got her a second ID. She said the money was her retirement fund."

"Did you ever meet this connection?"

"No, and I didn't want to. I think he was connected to her new boyfriend; a guy named Giulio. He scared me."

"Why did he scare you?" Tash asked.

Jeannine shrugged. "I'm not sure, you know how some guys give you a bad vibe? He was like that."

"Does Giulio have a last name?"

"Ah—Lupin, I think."

"What does he look like?"

"He's tall with curly blond hair and looks like he works out a lot."

"Anyone else you can think of?"

"Well, she ran with Jean Coudet's crew when we were younger. She still hung out with them sometimes. A woman in the

last office named Eve something. Eve
Covert, that was it. Simone arranged for
her to take the fall for the embezzlement
there. If she found out, she probably
holds a grudge."

"Okay." Judith rose. "Thank you for
helping us. If you need a reference for
an apartment or something, give me a
call."

Jeannine blinked in surprise.
"Thanks. You didn't need to say that,
though."

"I know I didn't. That's why I did."

"You like her," Tash said as they got
back into the sled.

"I did. Let's go see if we can locate
this Eve Covert."

"How?"

"Employment hiring records. It will
have the last place she worked. We can
probably find this Eve Covert by calling
Simone's last employer. Providing we can
get into the lab."

The police seal was still on the
front door of Dreamedia Laboratories.
However, workers were being allowed to
enter through the side door. Because

they had entered through a different door, Tash and Judith didn't start in the reception area. To reach it they had to travel the hall used by employees to the breakroom and employee lockers.

"We need to check in," Judith told Tash, heading for reception. The visitor greeting area held a desk of carved hardwood, polished to a deep sheen. It curved around the perky blond receptionist dressed in a low-cut blouse with enormous sleeves, cinched with a tight bustier, and skintight striped pants. several comfortable, overstuffed chairs for visitors lined the walls. A clear acrylic panel separated the reception area from the main office. Behind this were doors leading to the company labs.

"Hi, Carola," Judith said as she opened the door into reception.

"Judith!" the woman exclaimed. "Are you alright? How is your father? Have they released him yet?"

"I'm fine. Thanks for asking. Dad is home, but he's under house arrest so he can't come to work. This is my friend

Tash. Is it alright if we check something
in the personnel files?"

"I assume your father wants the
information, so I don't see why not. Do
you have the codes?"

"No, I don't," Judith admitted.

Carola tapped the desk com. "Yes?" a
voice answered.

"Isolde, Dr. Garney's daughter is
here. He wants her to look up something
in the personnel files."

"I'll be right out."

Isolde Botrel was a tall, slim woman,
with a pair of pince-nez spectacles
perched on her elegant nose.

"Miss Garneys it's good to see you
here. How is your father?"

"He's home but he's under house
arrest. Can we get a look at Simone's
personnel file?"

"Of course. You can have a copy of
what I gave the detectives. Follow me."

Isolde led the way through the maze
of desks to a door the back of the room.
She laid an empty crystal on a monitor
and asked for a copy of Simone Gusset's
personnel file.

"I'm sorry, I don't believe we've met," Isolde said, looking at Tash.

"Oh, I'm so sorry!" Judith exclaimed. "This is Tash Higgins from earth."

"I'm Devon Morton's assistant," Tash said.

Isolde frowned. "Devon Morton? I don't recognize the name."

"He's the Portal expert who came back from earth with Randal," Judith said, accepting the crystal and dropping it into her pocket.

"Is there anything else happening I should let Dad know about?"

"Nothing major. I'll send him an update about the progress on the Bradstane and Albyn projects later today."

As the two girls got into the carriage, Tash noticed another vehicle parked close to theirs. It was huge compared to Judith's carriage and resembled a sleek bird of prey. She glanced out the window as she closed the door.

Two burly men got out of the sled and were approaching their vehicle.

"Judith, do these doors have locks?"
she asked urgently.

Judith looked up from reading the
data contained on the crystal. "Yes,
it's that button there." She pointed to
a panel on the side of the carriage wall.
"Why?"

Tash quickly pushed the button and
the lock's clicked; She was barely in
time; as the doors locked, the two men
attempted to drag them open. "That's
why," Tash said grimly.

When the first attempt failed, they
yanked harder on the doors, rocking the
carriage.

"Let's get out of here," Tash said.

Judith tapped her wrist com. "Code
red," she said, "leave now!"

"My sensors say there are two
individuals close by who might be
damaged by this action," a robot voice
said. "Do you still wish to proceed?"

"Yes!" Judith snapped. "We are in
danger! Don't let those men enter the
vehicle!"

"As you command," The carriage
abruptly shot forward, throwing Judith

back against the seat and almost spilling Tash forward onto the floor. The two men hung on to the doors and were dragged several yards before they were forced to drop off.

Their would-be kidnappers scrambled to their feet and raced to their own vehicle, which took off in pursuit.

"They are following us," Tash said.

Judith tapped her com again, "Call Randal," she said.

A few seconds later, his face appeared as a holo vid. "Judith? What is it?"

"We just left the Lab. Two men tried to get into our carriage. We managed to lock them out, but they are following us."

"We're on our way to you. Did you instigate the security protocol?"

"I called a Code Red. It's what we use for emergencies," she said.

The sled following bumped them and the carriage jerked.

"They're playing bumper cars," Tash said. "How much armor does this thing have?"

"No more than ordinary," Randal said grimly. "Judith did you bring your pistol?"

"No, but Dad always has a couple in the carriage." She dropped the data crystal back into her pocket and reached under the seat, pulling out two plasma pistols. She handed one to Tash, who took it gingerly. Her sister's husband had made sure everyone in the family knew how to fire a variety of pistols, and these were like the ones issued to Police in Laughing Mountain.

The carriage jerked as the sled behind them hit it again.

"Okay," Randal's voice came out of the com unit. "I've got your location now. We'll be there in a few minutes. Is your driver equipped with combat protocols?"

"I don't know. I don't think so."

"Damn! Okay, you need to take manual control of the sled."

"Alright, I've got it," Judith said as a control wheel and console popped out of the floor. "Now what do I do?"

"This is a little tricky. Push the altitude level down and hit the brakes. Hopefully they'll sail right past you. Can you do that?"

"Okay, here goes nothing," Judith said. The big sled chasing them slid by overhead. Judith almost panicked when she realized the nose of her sled was still aimed at the ground. She pulled upward frantically on the control wheel attempting to level off the craft. Unfortunately, she had over controlled the command and their sled shot skyward.

It took her a few minutes to regain the proper altitude. When she had, she saw the two sleds ridden by Randal and Devon position themselves between the carriage and the pursuing sled. It looked like two falcons confronting an enormous raptor. Randal and Devon were mounted on sleek, fast, single passenger sleds shaped like falcons, The smaller sleds gave them more speed and maneuverability than the big raptor.

"We're here. While we engage the other sled, turn around and head for my parent's house."

"But—"

"I don't have time to argue about this Judith. Just do it!"

Judith cast a worried glance behind them but obeyed the order and headed for the Langeton home.

Randal had added a few modifications to the sleds used by his family. He squeezed a button on the handlebars and a plasma bolt shot toward the raptor shaped sled. It was a fair hit, tearing a hole in the side of the vehicle, but it didn't bring it down.

The recoil from the heavy plasma bolt nearly caused Randal's sled to turn turtle.

Taking warning from what happened when Randal fired, Devon shot his plasma bolt too, but when his sled tried to turn over on him, he turned into the circle, coming around to face the other sled again.

Nothing else was necessary. Devon's shot had hit the sled's power source, and it pancaked on the muggy ground below them.

Both men landed carefully near the wreckage and went to examine it.

"See if you can find out who it's registered to," Randal asked. He was searching the two men for identification.

"It looks like a corporation called Midnight Express owns this," Devon said. "Are they alive?"

"Yes, but both of them seem to be out cold," Randal replied, as a patrol sled slid to a halt beside them.

"What happened here?" the officer was an older man, probably close to retirement.

"It's a long story, officer," Randal said.

"Why don't you see if you can shorten it?"

"This vehicle attacked my fiancée and her friend as they were coming home from picking up some things for Judith's father. When it wouldn't back off, we fired at it."

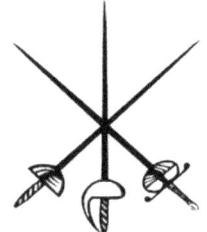

I CAPTURE THE CASTLE

DETECTIVES STRAUS and Addicock had listened to DaVinci's report about the threat to his family with skepticism. It wouldn't be the first time a defense attorney had attempted a little misdirection.

Straus, who was in the process of separating from his wife, got a frantic call a few hours later.

A strange woman had attempted to take his daughter out of school.

"What's going on, Con?" his soon-to-be ex-wife demanded. "The school called. Someone attempted to take Louise out of school. They said you sent them."

"What? No, I didn't send anyone. Is Louise safe?"

"Yes. She's waiting for me to come and pick her up."

"Let me make a few calls," he told her. "After you get her, pack a few things in case I need to send you to a safehouse."

"Alright," she said. "This sort of thing is why cops shouldn't get married!"

"What is it?" his partner asked.

"You remember Langeton's lawyer saying someone had threatened him after he arranged Langeton's bail hearing?"

"Yeah. I didn't think there was anything in it. You didn't either as I recall."

"Earlier today, someone tried to get my daughter out of school. They apparently said I sent them. I don't believe in coincidence,"

"Is she okay?"

"Yes. The school security is
pretty good. The woman wasn't on the
list of allowed contacts, so they
called my wife to verify it. Mathilde
called me. Adeline is waiting for her
in the principal's office. I need to
find a safe house for them until I
can figure out who is behind this."

"Why now?" Addicock wondered. "We
aren't involved in any high-profile
investigations…"

"Maybe we are," he said slowly.
"Didn't you say Randal Langeton told
you some type of top-secret data
crystal had gone missing?"

"I would have thought an attempt
to grab your daughter was to get back
at you for something you did in a
past case, not something we have
going on now."

"We'll look into both," the two
detectives turned as their Captain,
a woman named Maria Barbeau, a tall
slim person with greying hair spoke.

"That was quick," Straus said. "I just got the com from my wife about it."

She handed him a crystal and a set of key cards. "The keys to the safe house. Send them there until we get this straightened out."

The com on Addicock's desk shrilled. When she answered it, it was a patrolman nearing retirement. "Detective, are you investigating a case concerning Dreamedia Laboratories?"

"Yes," she said. "Why do you want to know?"

"Well, an attempt was made to kidnap Dr. Garney's daughter as she was leaving the lab with some information he asked for."

"Is she hurt?"

"I haven't spoken to her. Randal Langeton, her fiancé is here. He and Devon Morton stopped the attack. He sent his fiancée home."

"You said he broke it up? How?"

"Well, they shot down the sled chasing the girls. The driver and his buddy are on the way to Mercy Hospital."

"How badly are they hurt?"

"The medics said one of them had a concussion and the other one was unconscious but breathing."

"Thank you. We're sending a forensic team out to take in the evidence. Please stand by until they arrive."

She turned off the com and looked at Straus and Barbeau. "So much for coincidence," she said. "Maybe we better put anyone investigating this case on alert."

The Captain nodded. "I'll do that. You two get out there to question Judith Garneys and her friend."

They were delayed because they went to the Garneys home first. A robot server told them through the security screen: "Miss Judith is at her fiancé's place."

"I want to know what she was doing before they tried to snatch her," Straus said.

"Me too," Addicock agreed.

"The crime scene is on the way," Addicock said. "Let's swing by it."

Straus nodded abstractly. He was currently engaged in an acrimonious discussion with his wife about the safe

house. "Mathilde, I know it's inconvenient, but I hope it won't be for long. You'll be safe there. We can't afford a bodyguard service, you know that."

He winced at her answer. "Yes, I know your father can afford it, but—" at least promise me you'll stay at the house until he can get the bodyguards in place."

Addicock pretended she hadn't heard. She knew a big part of Straus's family issues stemmed from the fact his wife's family was wealthy and he only had his cop's salary.

Addicock and Straus arrived as Randal and Devon were mounting their sleds to leave.

"A moment please, Mr. Langeton," Addicock called.

Randal put his sled into park and waited for them. Neither he nor Devon turned off the motor.

"Was there something you wanted, detective?" Randal asked.

"Several things actually," Addicock said. "What happened here?"

"My fiancée and Tash Higgens came by
the lab offices to get some information
her father asked for. When they left,
the men in the sled tried to get into
their vehicle. When they couldn't they
followed them. The men in the sled ran
into them several times to force the
girls to land. I assume it was an attempt
to kidnap them."

"I see," she said. She glanced at
Straus who was still frowning at his com
link. "Why do you think someone would
attempt to kidnap your fiancée, Mr.
Langeton?"

"Judith told me she intended to speak
to Gusset's roommate today. Presumedly
someone is afraid she might have learned
something about who really murdered
Gusset."

"You're assuming neither your father
nor Miss Garneys killed her."

"They didn't," he said flatly.

"How do you know that?" she
challenged. "Were you there?"

"You know where I was," he replied.
"As I told the officer last night, a
valuable piece of data technology is

missing from the lab. Both my father and Professor Garney's had access to it. They would have had no reason to steal it. Simone Gusset was involved in a few illegal activities. I suggest you start looking into them instead of harassing innocent men."

"But you refuse to tell us what exactly is missing."

"Get clearance and I will. Until then, you don't need to know what it is, only that it's missing."

She stared back at him for a moment with her cop's stare. It usually worked to intimidate suspects. It failed today.

"If there is nothing else—"

"Actually, there is. An attempt was made to kidnap Detective Straus's daughter today. It could be a coincidence and not related to this case, but as your attorney reported being threatened as well…"

"I see," he replied. "I suggest you keep an eye on Gusset's roommate. She could be in danger as well. Now, if you don't mind, I need to check on Judith."

He put the sled in gear and sped off,
followed by Devon. Addicock stared after
the two men before she contacted her
captain to request a patrol sled check
out Gusset's apartment.

When Judith and Tash arrived at
Randal's home, they found Ava there.

"They let Dad come home," Ava told
her sister. "Mom and I've been looking
for you. Where were you?"

"Looking into a few things," Judith
replied. "We spoke to Simone's Gusset's
roommate. It turns out she's a cousin.
She gave us an earful about stuff Gusset
was into. It isn't good."

"Then they'll have to let Dad and
Professor Langeton go, won't they? They
have to see they're innocent."

"I'm beginning to think it isn't so
simple," Judith said. "A couple of guys
tried to grab Tash and I when we left
the lab today."

"Grab *you*? Why?"

"I don't know. Maybe Randal will have
a few ideas. He told us to come here."

"Allison finally fell asleep,"
Professor Langeton said from the

doorway. He looked tired and rumpled. "This has been hard on her. Did I hear you say someone tried to grab you girls?"

"Yes," Judith said. "Randal sent us here. I assume he's on his way."

"It might be a while," Tash said. "As we left, I saw both sleds fire at the one who tried to run us off the road. They might have to deal with the police about that."

A robot server brought in a tray loaded with small sandwiches, a coffee pot, and cups which she sat on a coffee table. "Shall I pour, Miss Judith?" she asked.

"Who ordered tea?" Judith asked.

"I did," Randal said. "Are either of you hurt?" he asked Judith. He didn't mention the gut-wrenching fear which had overtaken him when he realized the criminals were trying to kidnap her.

"I'm fine," Judith said impatiently.

"Tash?" Devon asked.

"We got a little banged up when they kept ramming us, but other than a few bruises, we're fine."

Randal came over to give his father a hug. "How's Mom?" he asked.

"I put her to bed and gave her a sedative. She didn't sleep last night," he said.

Judith lifted the pot to pour the coffee. Tash took hers and a small sandwich.

"I think it's time someone told us what is going on," she announced. She fixed Randal with a severe eye. "This isn't only about the stolen data crystal, is it?"

"Well, it's a big part of it," he said. "But you're correct, it isn't all of it."

Judith glared at him. "You joined them, didn't you? The Black Templars. They're the ones who insisted Dad and the Professor keep Gusset on the payroll after she tried her blackmail stunt, aren't they?"

Everyone except Professor Langeton looked at her.

"What, or who are the Black Templars?" Tash asked.

"Better tell her son," Randal's father advised.

He scowled. "Alright, but none of you can repeat this. Yes, Judith, I was invited to join the Templars. They're the ones who sent me to earth with the virus to protect our colony from being discovered." He looked at his father. "The rest is your story."

"Yes. Well, as it happens Agustin and I are also members. A few months ago, we were asked to employ a lab tech named Simone Gusset because they wanted to keep an eye on her. They think—thought she was a member of an organized crime ring involved in a lot of criminal activities."

"What activities," Judith demanded.

"Well blackmail, obviously, embezzlement, grifting and scams, even a few designer drugs."

"Were you supposed to allow her to embezzle your company? To blackmail you?" demanded Allison. She had followed her husband.

"I thought you were going to sleep a little," he said.

"No, you wanted me to sleep, Timothy.
I never said I would. I'm not a child!
I'm your wife! I have a right to know
what is going on."

He sighed. "Yes, you do."

"I think all of us want to know, Dad,"
Randal said.

"I had already told Mathieu I
intended to pull the plug on the
operation. Agustin and I didn't mind
helping out with their investigation,
but we weren't going to allow her to
steal from us or ruin our marriages."

"Do the police know any of this?" Ava
asked.

"I don't know," Timothy Langeton
replied.

"Judging from my conversation with
those two detectives, I'm betting
they've been told squat," Randal said.

"There's something else," Timothy
Langeton said. "Mathieu told me today
there has been a series of
disappearances. All those who vanished
have relatives connected with
investigations of a crime cabal called
the Red Conclave. When we reviewed the

investigations, all of them seem to have stalled. The templars think the conclave is keeping the missing people somewhere as hostages for their relative's behavior."

"I want a list of who's vanished," Randal said.

"I'll see if I can get you one," his father said.

NO COUNTRY FOR OLD MEN

JUDITH PULLED out her com and punched buttons. "Who are you comming?" Randal asked.

"Jeannine Silverton. I want to warn her."

Randal frowned. "Are you sure she's not involved?"

"Well, not a hundred percent sure," Judith admitted, "but sure enough I think she deserves a warning to be careful."

"She was in a position to know a lot about what Simone was doing. More than she told us, I'm sure." Tash added.

Judith frowned when no one answered the com. "I'm sorry," the return message said, "but the party you are contacting is not available at this time. Would you like to leave a message for her?"

"Yes. Jeannine this is Judith Garneys. A couple of toughs tried to grab Tash and I on the way home from your apartment. They might try for you as well. Please be careful and get in touch with me if you need help."

As it happened, Judith's warning came too late. Jeannine had already decided she needed to get out of town. She had been packing when Judith and Tash arrived. She commed for a sled taxi and gathered what she intended to take with her. When she heard a vehicle drive up, she opened the door and froze.

"Going somewhere?" Giulio Lupin asked.

"Yes, I'm going home for Simone's
funeral," she said.

"I don't think so," he told her.
"The boss wants to talk to you."

A chill ran down the girl's back,
and she kept her voice steady with an
effort. "Why does he want to talk to
me? I don't know what Simone was
into. I just finished telling that to
Professor Garney's daughter. Simone
was good at keeping secrets."

She started to step back into the
apartment, and he gripped her arm.
"Not so fast. The sled is over there.
Let's go."

Jeannine dropped the things she
had intended to take and kicked him
hard in the shins.

"Bitch!" he said. He slapped her
across the face and yanked her out
the door. Leaving it open, he dragged
her to the sled and threw her inside.
She tried to scramble back out, but
the man sitting in the seat grabbed

her. She felt the sting of a pressure syringe and the world went dark.

The sled taxi she had called arrived as they were pulling out. The driver, a woman with many years of experience in her profession, looked over the situation, the wide-open door, the spilled luggage and the hastily departing sled and drew her own conclusions. She commed her dispatcher and asked if she should report what she saw.

"I'll report it," she was told. She shrugged and went to her next fare.

"I don't like it," Judith said. "Tash, I think we should go check on her."

"You'll do no such thing," Randal declared. He had no desire to re-experience the blind fear he had felt earlier. He glared at her. "Did you forget someone just tried to grab you? You need to stay here where it's safe!"

"I'll go armed this time," Judith snapped. "My father is in trouble too. I'm not going to sit on my hands and wait for someone to come help us!"

Randal glared at her. "You'll do what you're told!"

Licorice, disturbed by the angry voices, climbed up Judith, making little anxious noises. She lifted him to cuddle him, keeping her voice calm with an effort.

"No, I will do as I think best. Besides, if I get taken maybe you'll find someone you like better to marry." She stood up. "Tash, are you coming?"

"I'm your wingwoman," Tash said. "Did you say you had pistols for us?"

"Tash!" Devon protested.

She blew him a kiss and followed Judith out of the room.

Judith's accusation had floored Randal. "Someone I like better?" he asked. "What the Hell is she talking

about? And that's no reason to go sticking her neck out like this anyway."

"How do you plan to stop her?" his father inquired.

"I can lock her in her room," Randal said furiously, heading for the door.

"It sounds to me as if you've got some fences to mend there," the elder Langeton said. "Maybe if you do, you'll get more cooperation."

"Well, whatever you were going to do, you won't do it here," Devon observed as a pair of one-man sleds sped by the window. "Unless I'm mistaken, there went our sleds. Maybe we should follow them to make sure they don't find any trouble."

"The door's wide open," Tash said when they arrived in front of the apartment.

"She must have been going someplace," Judith said. "But why leave her luggage behind?"

Maybe she didn't have a choice,"
Tash said. "It looks as if the
suitcases have been searched." A
high-pitched yip sounded from
somewhere in the jumbled pile of
suitcases. "What's that?" she asked.
"Did she have a pet?"

"Maybe," Judith answered. "See if
you can find it while I make sure she
isn't lying hurt inside."

Unpiling the opened suitcases,
Tash found a soft-sided animal crate
with a screen for air. She unfastened
the door, and a catamount popped out.
Licorice was blue grey; this one was
almost lavender with a pink nose and
pink-tipped ears. The creature leaped
into her arms, climbing her shirt,
and making distressed noises.

"Sssh," Tash crooned. "It's going
to be okay. You can stay with me until
we find Jeannine." The catamount wore
a tiny silver locket on her collar.
Tash tapped it, and it said, "Hi, my
name is Fidget. I belong to Simone

Gusset. Her com number is 213859. If I am alone, please com her so she can come and get me."

"No one else is here but us," Judith reported, coming back. "but the place has been trashed. So, either she ran away, or someone took her."

"This is Fidget. Her collar tag says she belonged to Simone. Are you going to report Jeannine is missing?"

"I guess we'd better," Judith said.

"We already know," Detective Straus said from the doorway. "The taxi dispatcher Jeannine commed reported it when the driver said no one was here. How did you girls get in?"

"The door was open," Judith said. "We were afraid Jeannine might be lying hurt in here, especially after we found that," She pointed at the opened suitcases.

"You do get around," Serena Addicock said. "I take it Silverton is gone?"

"Yes," Judith replied. "For what it's worth I didn't see any blood."

"We'll need your DNA and fingerprints for exclusion," Addicock said in resignation.

Randal stewed about the argument all the way to Silverton's address. By the time he and Devon arrived, his temper had come to a rolling boil. He ignored the police sleds and a forensic team going through the apartment and stalked over to Judith.

"I ought to wring your neck," he told her. "Do you *want* to get kidnapped?"

Hands on her hips, Judith glared back at him. "No, of course I don't!"

"Ah, perhaps we could save this until later?" Tash intervened. "I'm sure Detectives Straus and Addicock have more important things to consider than our personal tiffs."

"The neighbor next door says a tall blond man forced her into a sled and drove off." It was one of the uniformed officers who spoke. He was young, fit and moderately good-looking.

Turning her shoulder to Randal, Judith asked, "Did she hear a name? Officer Hawtree?"

"According to Mrs. Sommelier, he only said 'the boss wanted to see her'," he replied, smiling at her.

"If you don't need my fiancée for anything else, we need to get back to the house," Randal said with icy precision.

Judith looked at him in surprise. A year ago, she would have hoped he was jealous another man obviously found her attractive, now she put it down to temper at disobeying his orders.

"Not my call," Hawtree said with regret. "I don't suppose I could

treat you to a cup of coffee later, Miss Garneys?"

"Com me and we'll talk about it," Judith told him with a smile. She turned to Addicock, "Detective, the catamount belonged to Simone. Since Jeannine isn't here, will it be alright if we take it with us?"

"I don't see why not," Addicock replied. She lifted the empty animal crate and handed it to Tash who was still cuddling Fidget. "You're probably going to need this."

"Thank you," Tash said. "I wasn't sure if it was okay to take it, but it does have her food and dishes."

"We'll see you back at the house," Judith said over her shoulder, giving Hawtree a smile as they mounted their sleds and left.

Exasperated, Randal glared after her.

"Man, are *you* in the doghouse," Devon said. "Maybe your dad's right about mending fences with her."

Randal turned to the two detectives. "Is anyone else missing? Should I warn our lab workers?"

"Perhaps you should," Straus agreed.

By the time Randal and Devon arrived back at the Langeton house after stopping at the lab to warn his employees, Judith and Ava had gone home and Tash was busy coaxing Fidget to eat.

Devon squatted next to them. "Does she need to see a vet?" He asked.

"She wasn't hurt, just scared." She leaned back against the sofa seat, stroking Fidget's soft skin.

Watching her face, Devon said, "You want to keep her, don't you?"

"Yes. Does it show, " she asked.

"To someone who knows you as well as I do, it does. You aren't quite as much of a softie as Tally, but you come close."

"How much trouble is it going to cause if I take her back with us?"

He shrugged. "We'll figure something out. She looks a little like those hairless cats; Miniskin I think they're called. Maybe we can get away with telling everyone she's a new variety."

After dinner, Randal's father asked to speak to him alone.

Devon had his nose buried in the codes on the data crystal he had retrieved from the potted plant at Dreamedia. He didn't even look up when they left.

"We need to talk son," he said.

"About what?"

"I couldn't help watching you and Judith today and it occurred to me seven months was a long time to be gone. I need to know if you still intend to marry her."

"Why are you asking me such a thing?"

"Because it looked to me as if you're trying to make her angry enough to break off the engagement."

"I gave my word I'd marry her. I'll keep it."

The elder Langeton frowned. "That isn't good enough. Son, none of us wants the two of you to get married and be unhappy. Look if you fell for someone on earth, Augustine and I'll work something out—"

"I don't cheat!" his son snapped.

"I know that. But I also know feelings don't always obey our will. Are you in love with Judith?"

"Of course, I care about her—"

"There is a big difference between being fond of someone and loving them enough for marriage."

"I know that. I don't know what got into her tonight. Why would she say I can look for someone to marry I'll like better?"

"Maybe she doesn't think you love her."

"Is that what you meant by mending fences?"

"I know I'm meddling in your affairs to say this, but if you intend to marry Judith, you better start doing some heavy courting. From what I saw this afternoon, I'd lay odds she's getting ready to call it off."

Randal was taken aback. "Courting? I spend time with her."

His father shook his head in despair. "How Allison and I gave birth to a child with so little understanding escapes me. How much time have the pair of you spent alone since you got back?"

"I've only been home a couple of days and there's been a lot going on—"

"Did you even kiss her the first time you saw each other again?" His father continued ruthlessly.

Randal was beginning to feel cornered. "Well, we were in public —
"

Timothy Langeton made a rude noise. "It wouldn't have stopped me if I'd been away from your mother for seven months. No wonder the girl thinks you don't love her!"

Randal threw up his hands in surrender. "Fine, I'll put in more effort."

"That isn't what I meant, and you know it," his father said. "Women are perceptive that way. If you don't mean it, she'll know. I think you need to examine your own feelings on this."

When Timothy Langeton left the room, his son stared out the window at the gorgeous view of the back patio dock, not seeing the colorful display of flowers or the brightly hued birds who made nests there. His father was right, he thought. His feelings for Judith seemed to have changed since the Party where Tash had been doped. She wasn't just his childhood playmate who would marry

him sometime in the distant future.
She was a beautiful, desirable woman.
Judging by that young policeman's
reaction this afternoon, a lot of men
thought the same. It was time he did
something about that.

Devon poked his head into the
room. "The good news is the copy is
usable," he said. We can work with it
until we recover the original."

"What? Oh, right. That's good
news. Did you tell Dad?"

"Yes. He has the copy now. What's
the matter?"

"My meddling parents. Dad gave me
a lecture about neglecting Judith. He
thinks she is about ready to call off
the engagement."

"Is that what you want?"

"You're the second person tonight
to ask me that question. No, I *don't*
want to break off the engagement. The
city sponsors moonlight gondola tour
through the city. Want to do a double
date tonight?"

"Sure, I'm game. I think Tash would like it. But a double date isn't exactly the right forum for a romantic evening. Maybe you and Judith should get a private gondola instead of dragging us along."

I KNOW WHAT YOU DID

"WHAT DO I wear for a gondola sight-seeing trip?" Tash asked Judith.

"Well, it's a boat, so no skirt. Casual clothing should be fine."

That evening the four of them waited in line with six other couples on the gondola rental dock. The boats were different sizes, some only held one or two benches for passengers. Others were clearly meant for large groups. The boats themselves were narrow flat-bottomed craft whose low sides were barely high enough to prevent waves from coming in the boat. A colorfully dressed robot gondolier stood in the back of the boat manning the sculling oar. Folded behind the passenger seating was a roof the Gondolier could raise in inclement weather. As they waited, another robot, also colorfully dressed, acting as concierge came along the line asking each group what type of ride they were interested in, and how many people in each party.

The group ahead of them was a large one—about six people, They were all laughing and talking, handing around a beverage of some sort. One of the men, apparently a little worse for the liquor he had been drinking, nearly fell into the water trying to board the craft. If one of the others hadn't caught the back of his doublet as he careened towards the other side of the boat, he would have tripped and gone overboard.

When the concierge reached their group, Randal and Devon stepped aside with him.

When it was their turn to step into the boat, Tash noticed it only had seating for two. "We need four seats, don't we?" she whispered to Devon.

"Not this time," he said, stepping into the craft. "Randal decided he needs some couple-time with Judith."

"Is he planning to grovel?" Tash whispered, keeping her voice low so Judith and Randal who were boarding the Gondola behind them couldn't hear what she said.

"Probably," Devon agreed. "Do you think he needs to?"

"Oh, yeah, big time," Tash said with a grin, as the concierge helped her into the boat and handed her a tiny life vest. "For your Catamount," he said. "Would you like me to show you how to put it on her?"

"It looks simple enough, I think I can manage it," Tash said, inserting Fidget's front legs through the arm holes and fastening the Velcro closure strips over her back.

As soon as they were seated on the wide padded bench, their Gondolier poled away from the dock.

"The buildings on this part of the ride were designed to resemble those in the City of Venice on earth," The Gondolier announced.

Devon leaned back on the bench, putting an arm around Tash.

"Would you like some traditional music?" the Gondolier asked.

"Yes," Devon said. Immediately the soft sounds of a string harp accompanied their Gondolier's voice as he sang.

Back on the dock, Judith hesitated when she realized Tash and Devon were boarding a two-person boat. "Aren't they riding with us?" she asked.

"No, Devon and I both decided we need to spend some couple-time with our ladies."

She frowned at him but allowed him to assist her in stepping into the Craft. "Thank you," she said to the

concierge when he handed her
Licorice's life vest.

Randal had already told the
concierge he wanted a romantic
atmosphere, so as soon as they left
the dock, their Gondolier began to
sing, accompanied by the soft strings
of a harp,

When Randal reached for her hand,
she let him take it, but didn't
return the clasp.

"I think I need to apologize to
you," he said.

"Oh? For what exactly?"

"For yelling at you after you and
Tash were nearly kidnapped. It wasn't
your fault, I know that, but it
scared the life out of me for you to
be in such danger and I over-
reacted."

"Okay," she said after a moment.
"Apology accepted."

"Dad said he thought you were
getting ready to break our
engagement. Are you?"

"I'm thinking about it," she admitted.

"Is there someone else?"

"No," she said, shaking her head. "It's just—we don't seem to have the kind of feeling for each other engaged couples should have. I've thought for some time that our engagement was out of sight, out of mind for you while you were on earth, and it doesn't seem to have changed since you came back."

"That's probably my fault," Randal said. "Mom says I have absent-minded-professor syndrome. When I'm working on a problem, I tend to focus only on it, and ignore everything else. I'm sorry. If you're willing to give me another chance, I'll try to do better."

Judith absently stroked Licorice's head while she thought about it. "I don't want to break off the engagement," she said at last.

"But I don't want to go on the way we have been either."

Randal slid an arm around her back. "Does that mean you forgive me?"

"I suppose so," she said wryly.

When he tilted her chin up to kiss her, she allowed it, expecting the usual sisterly peck he always gave her. Instead, the arm around her shoulders tightened and his mouth became demanding. Startled, Judith gripped his shoulders, allowing the invasion of his tongue.

Having that intense focus turned on her was different—and exciting. Judith slid her arms around his neck and gave herself over to the feelings swamping her senses.

The narrow canals were barely wide enough for two boats to pass each other. Ahead of them the party boat, as Tash was coming to think of it, resounded with several voices singing. It came to a halt where

another canal crossed the one they were traveling on while the group argued as to which was the best way to go.

Tash and Devon's Gondolier, who had told them to call him Phillipe, perforce stopped their craft to wait for the passage to clear.

Tash looked over her shoulder. The Gondola Randal and Judith were using had halted as well, but since the pair were locked in an embrace, she doubted they noticed.

"Looks like groveling worked," she remarked, nodding at the craft behind them.

"I guess so," Devon agreed. "Umm—I don't need to do any, do I?"

"Do any what?"

"Groveling?"

She looked at him in astonishment. "For what?"

"Well after the duel—"

"Stop right there, Devon Morton," she held out a hand. "No woman wants a man to apologize for wanting to kiss her. If you try it, I'll—I'll push you into the water!"

He grinned at her. "Okay, was it good enough to do it again?"

"We won't know until we try it, will we?"

It was a gentler kiss this time, but as passionate. Fidget, bored with the human's mating rituals, jumped from the seat into the bottom of the boat, snagging her collar on the carved edge of the bench. In her struggle to free herself, she managed to break the delicate fob fastening her ID tag to her collar. The Gondolier's robot eyes and ears heard the small sound as the silver ID hit the bottom of the boat, and his eyes marked its location. He would retrieve it and return it to his passengers when he was less occupied.

The party boat finally decided on its route, allowing all the boats waiting behind it to finish their tours.

Arriving back at the dock an hour later, Tash and Devon's Gondolier stopped him as he climbed the steps onto the dock.

"Sir, I think your catamount lost this off her collar," the Gondolier said, handing the small silver disc to Devon.

Randal and Judith hadn't yet returned, so Devon and Tash sat on one of the waiting benches to wait for them.

"What's that?" Tash asked, looking at the disc.

"The Gondolier said it came off Fidget's collar. Let me see it and I'll try to reattach it."

She unbuckled the collar and handed it to him, watching as he lifted it to examine the catch. "Is the catch broken?"

"Yes," he said, "but there seems to be something else behind it."

He pulled out the jeweler's loupe he used to examine small circuitry and looked at the catch through it. "I think it's a second disc. Simone must have hidden it behind the ID tag, thinking no one would look for it there."

He put Fidget's collar into his pocket. "We'll look at it when we get back to the house."

Judith and Randal emerged from the Gondola holding hands.

"Well," Tash said with a smile, "that's an improvement."

"What? Oh, yes, I guess the groveling worked," Devon said, his mind on what could be on the new disc.

"As soon as Randal and Judith reached them, he jumped to his feet. "We need to get back to the house. Tash and I've found something behind the ID disc on Fidget's collar."

Randal glanced at Judith. "Do you mind? It could be important. We can order dinner in."

"No," she said smiling. "Some things never change; I'm as anxious to find out what Simone thought she needed to hide as you are."

When they returned, Langeton senior frowned at them. "You're back early. I thought you planned to go out to dinner."

"We did, but Devon and Tash found something hidden in Fidget's collar," Randal said.

"I hope you don't mind, but we ordered dinner brought in," Judith added. "We ordered enough for you and Allison as well."

Timothy Langeton's keen eyes studied her face, relaxing when he realized the tension had gone out of it.

He asked anyway, "Are you alright with breaking your date?"

"Yes," she agreed. "What's on the hidden disc might clear you and Daddy, so I'm as anxious to examine it as Randal is."

"Don't bother about us for dinner.
Your mother and I are enjoying the
spa," Langeton Senior said turning to
leave.

When the robot butler brought in
their takeout order, the four of them
were studying the information from
the disc. Simone Gusset had collected
a large amount of data on the Red
Conclave's activities and personnel.

"No wonder they got rid of her,"
Devon said, eying the sizeable files.
If the Red Conclave learned she was
collecting all this information, her
bosses must have been worried about
how she intended to use it."

"This looks like a record of
payments," Judith said, pointing at
several lines of credits. "Jeannine
thought her cousin was blackmailing
a few people. Maybe this is a record
of the payments she got."

Another spread sheet showed a list
of names. Attached to each name was

a record of what it was paying for. A third had a list of addresses.

When she read the information on the final spreadsheet, Judith said, "Oh, no, this is probably why she was killed."

Randal was frowning at the list of names. "Hold on, I want to check something," he said, pulling out the information his father had obtained from Mathieu Heroux. Besides a list of missing persons, it also had a list of suspected Red Conclave operatives attached.

"Everyone on this list is on one of Simone's spreadsheets," Tash said, reading over Devon's shoulder.

"All the address on here belong to the people on the lists, except the last one. What is Morthan Castle?" Judith asked.

"It's owned by the Lockton family," Randal said. "I think the present holder just inherited it. His name is Geoffrey Lockton."

HEIRS OF AVALON — BOOK 2 THE OUTLAW COLONIES

VALLEY OF SHADOWS

"WHAT DO WE know about these people? I mean is there a way for us to see if any of them have a criminal record or not? It would be a way to discover which of them are the victims." Devon said.

Randal nodded. "I'll feed the lists into the system and ask for background scans on them."

The butler entered the room, followed by a maid (also a robot) wheeling a tray with plates, cups and serving dishes. They proceeded to set dinner out on the buffet.

Randal had ordered the meal from a popular Oriental restaurant, and enticing smells wafted toward them.

"I'm hungry; Let's stop and eat before the food gets cold," Judith said practically.

While they ate, Randal's database chunked out surface backgrounds on each name.

"This is interesting," Devon said. "The people on this list are connected to the missing persons list your father came up with."

"Yes," Randal agreed, "and those on this one all seem to have had brushes with the law."

"If Simone was involved with the Red Conclave, why would she have a list of criminals?" Judith wondered.

"Maybe she was building a power base," Tash suggested.

"We need to talk to some of the people on this list," Randal tapped the list of victims. "In the morning, I'll hand the second disc off to Detective Addicock. They can run with it."

"Aren't you going to find out how the victims are connected?" Judith demanded.

"Of course, we are, but this second disc is evidence. We are legally required to turn it in."

"I've made copies of everything on it," Devon said. "Maybe we should com the detective tonight?"

"Okay," Randal pushed his sleeve back and tapped a code into his com link.

Addicock and Straus both came to collect the new evidence.

"She hid it in her catamount's collar?" Serena Addicock asked.

"Yes," Devon said. "We took one of those moonlight Gondola tours earlier this evening. Fidget got tangled in the bench seat and when she jerked free, she broke the latch holding her ID tag to the collar. When I tried to put it back on, I realized there was a second disc behind the ID tag. Quite clever really."

"She was clever alright," Addicock said sourly. "The more we look into her background the more illegal stuff we find."

"Does this mean our fathers can return to working in the lab?" Judith asked.

"Yes, they've been bumped way down on the list of suspects."

"Not to look a gift horse in the mouth," Randal Said, "but what changed your minds?"

Addicock looked at Straus, who shrugged. "Might as well tell them," he said.

"The course of the investigation has changed. We think more is going on than the theft of a data crystal."

"An attempt was made to take my daughter out of school," Straus added. "It failed, and fortunately, my ex-wife's father can afford a bodyguard for them."

"A lab tech from the police evidence section was told he'd better

lose the evidence on Gusset's murder. He was sent vids of his parents working in their garden."

Randal nodded. "I've been authorized to tell you the Black Templars don't think Gusset was murdered for the data crystal she was stealing, although receiving it was probably a bonus."

Addicock's eyes sharpened. "Oh? Why do they think she was murdered?"

He shrugged. "She was a member of the Red Conclave. The information on the disc we gave you will show she was collecting data about her bosses, presumably with an eye to using it to rise in the ranks. An investigation into her death could lead to exposing some of their activities."

"Excuse me, I need to report this," Addicock stepped away to com her Captain.

"If you don't mind a piece of advice, Detective, you might pull in Jean Coudet and some of the crowd he runs with. Gusset's cousin told Judith her cousin worked with them occasionally," Randal suggested.

"We've got to leave," Addicock came back. "Captain Barbeau just told me I've had a break-in at my place."

The two detectives left in a hurry.

"This is going to get nasty," Randal said. "Judith will the two of you *please* agree to stay here while Devon and I look into some things?"

"At least he said please this time," Tash offered.

"Okay, but I want to know where you're going and what you intend. If you disappear, I want to know where to come looking for you," Judith said.

"That could be more dangerous—"

"Shut up, and take the win," Devon said out of the side of his mouth. "It's probably as good as you're going to get."

"We're going to grab Coudet when he comes out of the Police station. I want to find out if he knows where they would have taken Silverton. Chances are, any other hostages are there as well."

As soon as Detectives Straus and Addicock arrived back at the precinct, they sent a couple of uniforms to pull in Coudet and Brunelleschi. When they arrived at the precinct, both men were a little worse for wear.

"What happened to them?" Captain Barbeau demanded. "You were told to bring them in, not beat them up."

They didn't want to come," Officer Hawtree said sullenly. "They weren't alone. The rest of the group is down in the holding cells being charged with assaulting a police officer and interfering with one in the performance of his duty."

Back at the Langeton house, Randal and Devon were getting ready to grab

Coudet, "Come with me. We need to get you the proper gear," Randal said.

Devon followed him into his room, fascinated to see the other man touch a seemingly blank panel. When he did so, a portion of the wall slid back to reveal an array of armor and weapons, all with the distinctive Black Templar emblem of a black gryphon on a gold background.

"Here," Randal pulled out two uniforms, handing one to Devon. "Put this on."

Devon stripped and slid on the pants and shirt. To his astonishment, the clothing shifted, fitting itself to his body. "Hey!" he said, "It's moving! Is it supposed to do that?"

"Yes," Randal replied, slipping his own shirt over his head. "It's body armor, too. Best to be had. The templars get it from Arcadia. I think it's made by our friend Mathias's father."

The last thing he handed Devon was a spare helmet, whose tinted faceplate obscured his features. "You won't need it until we grab Coudet," Randal said.

Both Judith and Tash were waiting at the door to see them off.

"Please be careful," Judith said, sliding her arms around Randal's neck to kiss him goodbye.

"You be careful too," Tash said. She eyed the form-fitting templar uniform. "That's quite an outfit. Does it have armor too?"

"It does," Devon assured her.

Devon and Randal waited outside the precinct in a large dark colored carriage Randal had borrowed from the Templars. He had also borrowed the two Mardi Gras masks now lying on the seat beside them. "We don't want them to be able to identify us," he had explained.

"No wish to be a stick in the mud," Devon remarked, "but if the police

can't get them to talk, what makes
you think we can?"

"The Templars have a place outside
of town for interrogations," Randal
said.

"You aren't thinking of torturing
them?"

"Physical discomfort isn't a
reliable method of interrogation,"
Randal replied. "The house does have
a supply of truth serum among other
things."

"Like what they gave Tash?"

"Similar, but this is legal. At
least I hope it is. You never can
tell when dealing with the Templars."

Coudet was scowling when he exited
the precinct. He was alone. He looked
around for his crew, but they were
still waiting in holding cells for a
bail hearing on the charges of
assaulting police officers and
interfering with one in the
performance of his duty.

When Randal and Devon stepped up on either side of him to each grab an arm, Coudet tried to dash back inside.

"Hey!" he yelled.

Devon heard the hiss of the pressure syringe Randal pressed against Coudet's neck. Coudet slumped between them.

"Pull his arm around your shoulder," Randal said, doing the same. Together they half carried Coudet to the waiting carriage. Once inside, Randal cuffed him to the seat and gave the order to head for Templar Headquarters.

The Black Templar headquarters chief attraction was its isolation. Sunderry basin was about ten miles from the city, located on the southern edge of the Grantois Lake, one of Barsoom's many freshwater tarns. This one rested within a volcanic caldera. Tributaries drained into it from the north and east and exited it via the Parkchester River which eventually made its way to the Southern Langstino Sea.

The building was a plain structure on the on the edge of Sunderry Basin. It looked like an ordinary farmhouse (well ordinary for Barsoom) surrounded on one side by Grantois Lake and on the others by farmland.

On their approach, Randal keyed in a code and hanger doors slid back revealing a cavernous space. He flew the sled inside and the doors slid closed behind him. Bright lights came on as they alit. Devon could see several other sleds of various sizes parked nearby.

Coudet wasn't completely unconscious; he was able to walk, but he did so drunkenly and required support.

Two robot servers brought a gurney to them and assisted Coudet onto it.

As soon as he was lying flat, a restraining field snapped into place.

"Interrogation room one please," Randal said, and the robots trundled off with the gurney.

An older man about forty, met them at the door of the next room. "Welcome home, Mr. Langeton," he said. "My compliments on your successful completion of your assignment."

"Thank you," Randal said. "This is Devon Morton, the Portal expert I told you about. Devon, this is Guillaume Peele, my boss."

"A pleasure to make your acquaintance, Mr. Morton," Peele said. "Who have you brought us, Mr. Langeton?"

"His name is Jean Coudet. I believe he knows where the missing hostages are being held."

"Why do you think that?"

"He was close to Simone Gusset, the Red Conclave operative who was

killed in Dad's Lab earlier this
week."

"And you brought him in because?"

"The Conclave is escalating their
activities; There have been at least
four attempts to kidnap the family
members of the police or anyone else
investigating Gusset's murder. They
succeeded in taking Gusset's cousin
and roommate Jeannine Silverton. One
of the attempts was on my fiancée and
a friend of hers. Devon and I foiled
it, and the two men are in custody,
but in no shape to talk. I believe
Coudet to be a low-ranking Conclave
member. He might not know a lot, but
since he was close to Gusset, I think
he might know more than he was
willing to tell the police when they
questioned him. I suspect he is too
frightened of his bosses to talk to
the police about the missing people."

Peele rubbed his hands together.
"Excellent. We'll see if we can be

more persuasive, shall we? I do love a well-done interrogation."

Randal rolled his eyes and followed Peele to the viewing interrogation room.

A one-way glass showed Coudet still on the gurney and one of the robots administering a drug in a pressure syringe, while the other stood by.

"I assume you both are acquainted with this gentleman since Mr. Morton fought a duel with him, so it would be best if you allow me to do the direct interrogation. You can watch from here."

"Yes, sir," Randal said. He sat in one of the comfortable observation chairs, gesturing for Devon to do the same.

Under the influence of the drug, Coudet talked. Not as much as Randal would have liked, but enough to confirm he was sure the hostages were being held at Morthan Castle.

"The robots can take him home while you contact those two detectives," Peele said.

"Straus and Addicock may want to speak to him in person," Randal said.

"Presumably, they know where he lives," Peele answered. "If the police want him, they can pick him up again."

"I'll ask them to meet us back at the house," Randal said. "Thank you, sir, for your help."

Peele chuckled. "No need to thank me, young man. I like to keep my hand in. It's been a while since I had the opportunity."

RAID ON MORTHAN

WHEN THEY returned to Randal's folks house, he immediately got on the com with Detective Addicock.

"We've had a tip on what is happening with the missing people," he told her.

"Who was your informant?" she asked.

"It came from someone in the Black Templars," he replied. "the person who told me about it wants to remain anonymous. Is this going to be a problem?"

"Hang on, I need to speak to my captain," she said.

Randal leaned back on the couch, accepting the cup of coffee Judith offered with a smile. "Thank you," he said.

"Did you learn anything from Coudet?" she asked.

"He thinks they are keeping the hostages at Morthan Castle."

"Why there?" Tash asked.

"Well, it's pretty isolated, so a steady influx of people arriving wouldn't be noticed."

"Do you think Geoffrey Lockton is a member of the Red Conclave?" Judith asked.

"Maybe. If the hostages are there, it could mean he's a member or it could mean they simply invaded his home and moved in on him."

"What do you know about him?" Devon asked.

Judith frowned. "I think he got married a year ago. I heard his wife just had a baby. She didn't go out much before she became pregnant, and of course she would have stayed home while she was carrying it."

"So how do we find out if he's one of the bad guys?" Devon asked.

"Detectives Straus and Addicock are here," the butler announced. "Shall I show them in?"

"Yes," Judith said, "And bring more coffee and cups please."

"Very good miss," he said.

Captain Barbeau was with the two detectives.

When Addicock introduced them, she nodded acknowledgement.

"Please sit down," Judith invited.

"I want to know more about this tip before I authorize any action," the captain said.

"It's reliable," Randal said. "Devon and I plan to do a reconnaissance tonight to make sure the missing people are actually there."

She frowned. "I see. What if you're caught?"

"Well, I was hoping your people would be standing by to go in if we confirm the hostages are being kept there."

"I see. I'll have to run this by my bosses," Captain Barbeau said. "Give me a couple of hours and I'll get back to you."

While they waited to hear back from Captain Barbeau, Judith dialed in an old spy vid from the 20th century on earth. The male lead was handsome and charismatic and the female beautiful. The hero and heroine had finally managed to destroy the villains' headquarters and defeat his attempt at world conquest when Barbeau finally got back to them.

"I managed to secure a search warrant for the castle," she said. "Since neither of you are actually police, Detectives Addicock and Straus will accompany you during your reconnaissance."

"That's fine," Randal replied, "but this is a Black Templar

operation until we can confirm the presence of the missing people. Your detectives will need to stay with the SWAT team until then."

"My bosses won't like that," she replied.

"Excuse me," a voice broke in and the vid com was abruptly transformed into a 3-way communication. "Perhaps I can help settle this jurisdictional dispute."

"Who the Hell are you, and how did you manage to get into this communication?" Barbeau demanded.

The person on the other end of the com wore a helmet with a faceplate covering her features. The crest on it was the distinctive Black Templar emblem of a black gryphon diving with its talons extended.

"My credentials," the speaker said, tapping a code into the com link. Immediately the same symbol popped up on the screen.

Barbeau scowled. "A moment if you please, I need to have my boss scan this."

"Of course," the voice said.

Barbeau's image was replaced by an older, dark-skinned, man whose bald head shone in the overhead lights,

"I'm Police Chief O'Connell," he said. I can confirm this will be a combined operation between the Templars and the Police. The Templars will take the lead in rescuing any missing persons being kept against their will at Castle Morthan. The Police will handle any investigation afterwards. Are we all agreed?"

"Yes Sir," Randal said.

Devon and Randal were once again dressed in the Templar uniforms. Before leaving for Morthan, they had gone by Templar headquarters and picked up the sleek, stealth equipped sled Randal now drove.

Morthan Castle was built on a hill sticking out of the quiet water in

the middle of Grantois Lake. The lake itself was in a caldera left by an ancient volcano. The hill occupied by Morthan Castle had been built on the site of a later eruption. In the moonlight Devon and Randal could see several skinny towers connected by dark red stones. On the left side, a precipitous cliff safeguarded access. "There's less likely to be security cams on the side with the cliffs," Randal said, bringing the sled to that side of the fortress.

"This is where they're keeping the captives?" Devon asked. "It looks like something out of a horror vid."

"This is the coordinates Coudet gave us."

"It's got a forcefield," Devon reported after examining it with the tiny scanner he had brought along.

"Can you disable it?"

"Maybe." A few minutes later, he announced, "Gotcha! I'm sending the

code to shut off the force field to
Straus and Addicock."

Randal's sled slipped inside the
edge of the force field. The Police
Sleds would wait outside in stealth
mode until they received a signal the
rescue operation was in process.

After he and Randal exited the
sled, Devon turned the force field
back on. "With luck, they'll think
their vid cam glitched," he said.

It was a slow slippery climb to
the back side of the castle. About
halfway up, Randal stumbled over
something warm and soft and alive. He
hit the ground hard. His nerves
weren't what they had been before his
father was arrested and an attempt
had been made to kidnap Judith. He
had a knife in his hand and was on to
him before he could get to his feet.

"Randal!" Devon hissed. "That's a
goat!"

"Dammit!" Randal said. He patted the goat on the head, "Sorry," he whispered.

After climbing to his feet, the goat appeared to consider matters before he left with a disdainful shake of his tail. Randal wondered why this sort of mishap didn't happen to the vid heroes in the action vid they had watched earlier.

He picked up his helmet, scowling as he looked out through the now cracked faceplate. "Can you see?" he asked Devon.

"What happened?"

"it looks like he stepped on the faceplate. It's cracked."

"It sure is. Does it still work?"

"It works, I just need to focus around the cracks."

They resumed their climb to the castle. Eventually the steep path leveled off, leaving about twenty feet to the edge of the rock-walled castle.

There was a guard. *Of course,
there would be a guard,* Randal
thought in exasperation. He touched
Devon on the shoulder and pointed.
Devon nodded.

The guard was walking away from
them as he made his patrol, but he
was bound to see them when he turned
around.

Devon lifted a handful of loose
pebbles from the path and tossed them
over the cliff. They made a
satisfactory noise as they bounced
off the interior of the forcefield
surrounding the castle.

The guard immediately went to peer
over the edge of the cliff,
suspecting someone was attempting to
scale it.

Randal and Devon were on him in a
rush, Randal grabbed him around the
neck, pressing his gun into the
guard's side. Devon grabbed the man's
pulse rifle and pistol, disarming
him.

"Now," Randal said, his voice echoing oddly from the misshapen helmet, "you're going to be a good boy and open the door for us."

The Guard, a man in his early twenties, with a nose already broken in some altercation, glared at them, and spat on the ground. "Go to Hell," he said.

"You first," Randal replied, dragging the man to the edge of the cliff. "How far down do you suppose it is?" he asked.

"Oh, maybe a hundred feet," Devon replied. "Do you think he'll survive the fall?"

"I doubt it," Randal said. "How much do you want to bet he does?"

"I can go for fifty—"

"Alright!" the guard said, sullenly. "I'll open the damn door."

"If an alarm goes off when we enter, we can still throw you off the cliff," Randal warned as the guard entered the code to open the door.

"It won't," the guard replied.
"I'm not that stupid."

"I sure hope not, for your sake,"
Randal said cheerfully.

Once inside, he instructed the
guide, "Now you're going to show us
where the prisoners are being held."

"It's this way," the guard pointed
a finger at the stairs leading into
the interior of the castle. "Old man
Lockton built some real good cells.
Guess he wanted this to look like a
real castle."

The path took them past the family
rooms. As they passed the library,
they heard voices.

"You sure got the poor end of the
deal," A man's voice said. "Instead
of attempting to figure out a way to
get you out of this, your dear hubby
is stinking drunk."

"He's only one man, against you
and the others!" a woman's voice
retorted. She sounded close to tears.
"He won't risk my life or his son's.

It's no wonder he gave in to despair."

"Sure, you keep thinking that," the other voice mocked.

Randal and Devon exchanged glances. The other voice had to be Thurston Albyn. They knew they couldn't afford to leave him behind with two potential hostages.

Randal handed off their prisoner to Devon and stepped into the room, and fired his pistol, stunning Albyn, who collapsed to the floor.

Mrs. Lockton let out a tiny scream.

The guard, seeing a chance to get away while Devon's attention was on what was going forward in the library, jerked away from him, and tried to dash down the stairs. Devon fired his pistol, hitting the man squarely in the buttocks. The guard collapsed, unconscious.

"Well, Damn," Randal said. "We needed one of them awake to show us where the other guards are and where prisoners are being kept."

"I think he only had about three men here," Mrs. Lockton said. "The others took off this morning for somewhere."

She rose and went to her husband, shaking his shoulder. "Geoffrey, you need to get up to show these men the guard rooms."

He peered at her owlishly, "What? Sorry, my dear, I'm a useless idiot. Thurston's right: you made a bad bargain."

"A moment if you will, please, Mrs. Lockton," Randal said. He opened a small pouch on his uniform and selected a vial. Unscrewing the vial, he poured it ruthlessly down Lockton's throat.

Lockton gasped and coughed. He slid out of his chair to his hands and knees, breathing like a freight train. "What the Hell was that?" he managed when he could speak.

"It's called Sober Up," Randal said. "Can you stand?"

"Yes," Lockton said, grabbing the arm of the chair to push himself to his feet. He looked down at Albyn and kicked him. "What happened to him?" he asked.

"I stunned him," Randal said. "The police are outside with a SWAT rescue team, but before I signal them, I need to get the rest of Albyn's men. Do you know where they are?"

"Probably in the guard barracks, playing cards," Lockton said. He pointed to Albyn, and the guard Devon had pulled into the room. "What about them?"

"Give me a pistol and I'll make sure they don't go anywhere," Mrs. Lockton said.

Devon handed her Albyn's pistol. "Here, you may as well use his," he said. He piled the guard's rifle on the library table and handed the other pistol to Lockton.

"They should be out for a couple
of hours," Randal told her.
"Hopefully, we'll be done by then."

"Thank you," Lockton said. "I
don't know who you are but thank
you."

"Courtesy of the Black Templars,"
Randal said. "Let's go find those
guards."

The three remaining guards were
indeed engaged in a card game. When
they saw the armed trio in the
doorway, one of them attempted to
draw a weapon, and Geoffrey Lockton
shot him.

The other two men raised their
hands in surrender.

"Where are the keys to the prison
cells?" Randal asked.

"He had them," one of the guards
pointed to the man Lockton had
killed.

"Back away," Randal ordered, as
Devon searched the fallen guard.

He found a small crystal on a chain. "Is this it?"

"Yes," one of them said.

"Shut up!" his colleague hissed. "We don't talk, or we'll get killed, remember?"

"I'm turning off the forcefield," Devon said. "Do you want me to let Straus and the rescue team know?"

"Do it," Randal said.

When the SWAT team arrived, not much was left for them to do except take Albyn and his men into custody. A medical team followed them in and were soon busy administering whatever medical attention the hostages needed.

Jeannine Silverton approached Randal and Devon who were about to leave. "She sent you, didn't she?" she asked.

"Who?" Randal asked.

"Judith Garneys. She's the only one I can think of who would have looked for me," she said.

"Then you need to thank her when
they get through with you," Randal
said.

SEVEN DEGREES OF SEPARATION

Seeing the police had the situation at Morthan Castle well in hand, Randal and Devon left. When they dropped off the sled at Templar headquarters, Peele met them in the hanger.

"Well done, gentlemen," he said. "Please join me in the library for a de-briefing."

"Me too?" Devon asked. "You know I'm not a member?"

"That isn't an issue," he was told. "Mr. Langeton requested you be given honorary member status for your stay on Barsoom."

Devon relaxed. "Okay, thank you."

A robot served them brandy in sniffer goblets as soon as they had taken chairs

"Begin download," Peele ordered and a vid from each man's helmet appeared on a split screen showing the events from each man's point of view.

"I got most of it from your visor cameras," he said, "is there anything you'd like to add?"

"Can you cut out the part about the goat?" Randal asked.

Peele chuckled. "Afraid not; it merely shows we are human, my friend. A new helmet will be sent to you to replace the one stepped on by the goat."

"Thurston Albyn is high-up in the Conclave Council, It will be a pleasure to interrogate *him*," Peele continued.

"What's going to happen to Lockton and his wife?" Devon asked.

"Well, they were as much victims as any of the captured hostages. I am going to suggest Lockton add some additional security to prevent this happening again."

"Since some of the hostages were related to police personnel, They have an issue of compromised evidence. Everything processed by those techs related to the hostages will have to be re-examined. I'm glad I won't have to be a part of that."

Jeannine Silverton came to call on Judith after she was released by the Police. "Thank you," she said. "The two operatives from the Templars wouldn't admit it, but I know it had to be you who turned in the missing person report on me."

"Are you alright?" Judith asked her.

"Yes. I was expecting to be interrogated, but I guess Albyn didn't have time. I see you found Fidget."

"Yes, I did," Tash admitted. "Her collar said she belonged to Simone. Are you here to reclaim her?"

"Actually no, but I suppose I should. I never understood why Simone got her in the first place. She wasn't a pet person. I'm not much of one either to tell the truth."

"If you don't want her, I'd be glad to take her," Tash said.

"Are you sure?"

"Yes, I'm sure," Tash cuddled the catamount, who purred in her ear.

"I'll send you the transfer of ownership papers," Jeannine said.

"What will you do now?" Judith asked her.

"I'm going home for Simone's funeral, and then I guess I'll be job and apartment hunting," Jeannine said.

"Dreamedia has a clerical position open. Why don't you apply for it?" Judith suggested.

Jeannine looked doubtful. "Would they hire me after what my cousin did?"

"You aren't your cousin," Judith replied.

"Okay, thanks. I'll send those transfer papers right along," she said when she left.

"Well," Judith said, "It looks as if you now own a Catamount."

"At least she's small enough to travel with me," Tash said.

"Where do you and Devon go next?"

"He has a meeting with Carter Willis, the Barsoom liaison to the other colonies to discuss importing Gregor's crystals. Afterwards, we will spend a few weeks in Laughing Mountain, After

that we'll move on to Arcadia and Lemuria. Devon told me he plans to spend a month on St. Antoni. I'll be able to visit with Tally and see how much my nieces and nephews have grown."

"How are you and Devon?"

Tash made a face. "He isn't sure I know my own mind. I suppose I can't blame him—I spent years thinking he was just a friend. It's going to take time to convince him I do love him. Are you and Randal doing better?"

"We had a good talk the night we rode in the Gondolas. We've agreed to try again. I understand him a little better, I think. He tends to develop tunnel vision when he's involved in something. I have to quit being afraid to remind him I expect him to pay attention to me as well."

"So, when is the wedding?"

"In about six months. I hope you and Devon will be able to return here for it."

"I'll make sure we do," Tash promised.

The day they were due to return to Laughing Mountain, Tash and Devon met Carter Willis, Barsoom's Liaison in his office. They were both acquainted with him, as he often made trips to earth. Willis had long black hair, worn in a man bun, and skin darkened by exposure to Barsoom's tropical sun.

"So, this is your lovely assistant," he said smiling at Tash. "Welcome to our colony, Miss Higgins."

"Call me Tash, please," she said. "Miss Higgins sounds too formal. I understand you have some questions about the Portals?"

"I do," he said, gesturing for them to be seated.

"Will it cause an issue if we set up a second Portal directly with Arcadia and the other colonies?"

"Theoretically, it shouldn't," Devon said, "but you understand it will be better if the two Portals aren't open at the same times."

"Even if they are connected to a different place?"

"As I said, this is theoretical, but I do know Earth-Gov operates multiple Portals. However, they have been careful to avoid having more than one open at a time."

"You're saying we will need to shut off the Portal at the mines while the one with Laughing Mountain is open."

"It's what I would recommend," Devon said. "Laughing Mountain only opens the connection to Barsoom once a month for short periods to allow the exchange of mail pouches, and only every three months for a longer period while more goods and services are sent through."

"I understand you have contracts for Arcadia and Lemuria to examine concerning importing the Gregor Crystals. We'll be happy to take them with us. We'll take a few days off in Laughing Mountain, but our next stops are Arcadia and Lemuria."

"I'll get them for you."

EARTH: OTHERWORLD GATEWAY

EARTH SURVIVED the multitude of physical and social disasters leading to the apocalypse. Contrary to popular expectations, the Apocalypse didn't arrive with a single incident such as a massive asteroid strike from space. Instead, it crept up slowly on earth's people. They endured the slow, incremental slide into world-wide catastrophe. The United States, Canada and much of Europe, had programs for disasters in place of course, but these contingencies had not been designed for world-wide emergencies lasting for years. As the series of disasters multiplied, many governments simply ran out of funding to continue them. The political structure of many nations, already in turmoil came under attack and in danger of collapsing.

A series of pandemic viruses the authorities seemed unable to check swept over the planet. The Draconian measures used to stop the spread of plagues further damaged the global economy. Businesses who were required to shut down or drastically cut back on their workforce simply didn't survive. When the pandemics were accompanied by global-wide earthquakes and volcano eruptions, many governments simply collapsed. What took their place was anarchy, rioting and urban warfare.

Scientists had predicted for years the tectonic plates holding the continents in position were due to move. No one had believed this was imminent until it happened. The Pacific Rim of Fire was the first; massive eruptions of the volcanos around the rim set off earthquakes along the three main fault lines running down the spine of the Americas. This caused widespread destruction followed by massive Tsunamis.

North America and parts of Europe had declared Martial Law, keeping a semblance of their former governments intact, albeit with some radical changes. Armed government soldiers did their best to help beleaguered police departments keep order in the large cities, where gangs of loosely unified 'protesters' periodically organized marches invariably leading to rioting, looting. and destruction of businesses, homes, autos, and anything else they could find to take out their simmering anger on.

In more rural areas, the fiercely independent citizen's militia groups protected citizens from both the government agencies who seemed more interested in sweeping aside citizens' rights than protecting them, and from the spread of criminal gangs who were fighting for control of the cities.

Thus, matters stood when scientists discovered a way to escape to another world by opening a planet-based wormhole the scientists dubbed a Portal. The fact was it took relatively little energy to power a gate, making taking advantage of these new-found worlds doubly attractive to government and industry. Prospective settlers lined up in droves to emigrate to these new worlds, and much money was made providing access and supplies for the new colonies.

Eager to restore their crumbling economies, Earth governments and industry banded together to control knowledge of Portal Technology, creating the Portal Settlement Acts. Generating a portal didn't require a lot of scientific knowledge and despite attempts to regulate the information about how to make a gate, Portals sprung up like fleas on a dog in summer. A

mishmash of different smuggling rings,
eager to supply the illicit colonies
with badly needed tech, supplies and
just about anything else they needed or
wanted, jumped into the fray.

An uneasy alliance developed between
the smugglers and the militia, who were
anti-government control, and fiercely
protective of citizen's rights. These
groups resented the Portal Settlement
Acts on general principal and were
disposed to help circumvent the agents
assigned to enforce them.

Desperate to stop the flow of money
slipping away, Earth governments
created the Portal Authority to combat
the smugglers. Its agents held powers
like those of police and military
authority to investigate and arrest
violators of the Act. The act itself and
the behavior of the first agents
enforcing it created fertile ground for
rebellion.

The isolation of the smaller towns
and settlements had helped prevent the

spread of the pandemics, and communities such as Laughing Mountain had taken steps to prevent the spread of the social unrest plaguing their brethren in the larger cities. In these small rural communities, life had gone on much as usual. People worked, grew food to feed themselves and their neighbors and children attended school. No one talked about the Portal Gate outside of town, or the flow of traffic going through it every month. Laughing Mountain was a bastion of rebellion, being the site of an illegal portal. This small mountain town lay about an hour's drive from the rebuilt city of San Demos. The high-priced homes of the rich and famous who lived there were slowly being rebuilt as governments regained some control of the cities. Martial Law was slowly being phased out of urban areas.

Gradually, the rich and famous returned to rebuild cities along the new coastlines, bringing their money and

idle lifestyles back to the areas they
had abandoned. They often spent an idle
afternoon shopping in the small
mountain towns, followed by lunch or tea
at the boutique cafe's catering to their
trade.

The Portal in Laughing Mountain was a
gateway to more than one colony. Besides
St. Antoni, the town had connections
with five other outlawed colonies.
Barsoom* (named after the planet in ERB
Martian books). Although the colonists
there claimed to want to live in the
style of the renaissance, they were much
too fond of their high-tech gadgets to
give them up. Unlike St. Antoni, this
colony was deliberately developed so
they would have control of their
connection with earth.

This was also true of both the
colonies of Arcadia and of Shangri-La;
one of whom was a socialist society and
the other a military dictatorship.
Halcyon, the last colony to be

developed, was created as a haven for Clones in response to blackmail,

Unlike new citizens of earth's official colonies, or the illegal planned ones, immigrants to St. Antoni had only the technology they could carry with them when they slipped through a portal. What they brought with them was their only defense against the alien plants and bizarre animals found on their new worlds.

BARSOOM*

GENERAL DESCRIPTION

The Planet itself is well within earth normal standards as far as temperature. It has two moons who orbit close together. Their combined mass is approximately 1½ the size Earth's moon. The planet has nine continents, the majority of which are scattered along the equator, with 68% of it water. It takes 425 days to orbit the sun, and each day is 27 hours. The colonists use the Greek Calendar in naming the months, with each month being approximately 35 days.

The Portal opened close to the equator. The city of Savano where the Portal is located, has been built to withstand the predations of tropical, fast-growing plants, and extreme humidity (it rains nearly every day). The colony is troubled by insects so they Cultivate the Lint Dragons to assist with bug control. Farmlands have been cleared and the soil is fertile, but the crops are under constant attack by native plants.

HISTORY

What if the d'Medici's and Borgias, or artists such as *Raffaello (Raphael) Sanzio da Urbino and Michelangelo, or scientists like Copernicus and Galileo had possessed advanced technology?*

The Outlaw Colony of Barsoom* was designed to be a mix of renaissance dress and manners coupled with advanced technology. By day, the colonists invent nanites to cure diseases and cast illusions. By night, they carouse in taverns and ballrooms served by robots. At dawn, they fight duels to the death over imagined or real insults.

Barsoom* (I received authorization to use the name from ERB, Inc. providing I give credit for the trademark to them in each novel) has the requisite two moons, but I'm giving it a tropical climate. Since their main industry is the manufacture of micro robots, stringent steps must be taken to prevent the deterioration of the robots.

Socially, Barsoom* enjoys a renaissance lifestyle. It was colonized by groups of people who wanted to recreate a renaissance culture but retain their technology. Colony organizers spent months sending through anything they thought they might need. Education level is high, main industries are researching and creating tiny robots called nanites which can be programmed for various medical, scientific instruments and weapons.

farming, fishing, merchants, mining, but since they love their high-tech gadgets, they also import many small circuits to make them with.

Since Barsoom employs Robots for many menial tasks, it doesn't have a 'noble' class system, but instead utilizes a more modern egalitarian way of classifying its population.

- A native of Barsoom should posses the qualities of good character, grace, and talents.
- A native of Barsoom should should be learned and should practice certain physical and military exercises.
- A native of Barsoom should have a classical education and should be able to play and instrument or be a proficient artist.

As mentioned before, Barsoom allows dueling. This is a highly stylized and organized method of settling individual disputes.

CODE DUELLO

Code Duello is a set of rules for a one-on-one combat, or <u>duel</u>. Code duello regulates dueling and thus helps prevent <u>vendettas</u> between families and other social factions. The code ensures a non-violent means of reaching an agreement, so harm be reduced, both by limiting the terms of engagement and by providing medical care. Finally, Code Duello ensures the proceedings have several witnesses. The witnesses are there to assure grieving members of factions of the fairness of the duel and provide testimony if legal authorities become involved.

A morally acceptable duel would start with the challenger issuing a traditional, public, personal grievance, based on an insult, directly to the single person who offended the challenger.

The challenged person had the choice of a public apology, other restitution or choosing the weapons for the duel. The challenger would then propose a place for the "field of honor". In the Capital city of Barsoom a field has been designated specifically for dueling. For a duel to be legal, participants must use this location which provides a judge to decide if the duel has been fair. The Dueling field also has rotating doctors on call to attend each duel.

Each side would have at least one second; two was the traditional number.
If one party failed to appear, he was considered a coward and the appearing party would win by default. The seconds (and sometimes the doctor) would bear witness to the cowardice. The resulting reputation for cowardice would often considerably affect the individual's standing in society, perhaps even extending to their family also.

The opponents agreed to duel to an agreed condition, either First Blood, Death or until either party was no longer able to fight, or the physician called a halt.
When the condition was achieved, the matter was considered settled with the

winner proving his point and the loser keeping his reputation for courage.

ANIMALS

LINT DRAGON: A small, warm blooded, four-legged winged mammal. It is covered in fine fur and resembles a floating ball of rainbow-colored lint. It is omnivorous with a diet consisting of berries, nuts, small insects, and grubs. Normally found in family groups consisting of several females and males of various ages and ranks and their fledglings. One dominant pair rules the others. some family groups will band with others to form a herd with one supreme pair who rules. Because of their small size (about the size of a hamster) they have few offensive weapons, but they do possess a painful sting. When a flock acts in unison to drive off a predator, their combined sting can cause injury or even death depending on the size of the predator. They can form a flock bond with a human, but only if they are socialized when they are young.

CATAMOUNT: small native mammal adopted by colonists as pets. It's about the size of

a Guinea pig. It looks hairless, but the
hair is so fine it's transparent. It has
large, bat-like ears, big eyes which change
in the dark. Hunts both during the day and
at night. It is Omnivorous with a diet of
fish, crustations, berries nuts and
occasional insects. Likes water, usually
found singly or in small family groups.
Adolescents move on when they reach
maturity. Can be fierce in defense of its
clan.

PLANTS

All flora on this world has an aggressive
growth pattern but so far, none of it has
proven actively dangerous to humans. It is
fast growing and will quickly take over a
field of crops if not kept under quick
control. This is mostly done with robots,
although the Barsoomians are quite
interested in genetically altering plant
species imported from earth to be strong
enough to hold their own with native flora.

The Outlawed Colonies series is a shoot off from the Forbidden Colony series. Each book is set on a different Colony reached through the same Portal serving St. Antoni. The colonies all have different social and cultural values. Forbidden to exist by Earth's Governments and the Industrial Giants who control the Portals, they manage to thrive under the noses of those agencies…

Learn More about the Forbidden Outlaw Colonies by following this link.

https://gaildaley.com/St-Antoni.php

ABOUT THE AUTHOR

A writer of Fantasy and Science Fiction stories, Gail has received high praise for her beautifully interlaced, imaginative worlds. She populates her universes with vital and interesting characters, skillfully intertwining their everyday lives with world changing events.

An omnivorous reader, she was inspired by her son, also a writer, to finish some of the incomplete novels she had begun over the years. She is heavily involved in local art groups and fills her time reading, writing, painting in acrylics, and spending time with her husband of 46 plus years.

Gail has a background in business and used this expertise to develop a series of pamphlets (lumped together under the title "The Modern Artist's Handbook) advising artists and authors about how to improve their bottom line by applying business practices to the development and sale of their work.

Currently her family is owned by two cats,
a mischievous young cat called Mab (after
the fairy queen of air and darkness) and
a mellow Gray Princess named Moonstone. In
the past, the family shared their home
with many dogs, cats, and a Guinea Pig,
all of whom have passed over the rainbow
bridge. A recent major surgery on her
stomach, a bout with breast cancer, and
arthritis in her hands have slowed her
down a little, but she continues to write
and paint.

www.gaildaley.com

A NOTE FROM GAIL

Thank you for reading this book. While each book was designed to be read without having read the prior volumes, Characters from prior books do appear in each story. This is the first book in the Outlaw Colony Series; The story will continue with a four more books.

I often get asked why I write. The answer is simple. I write books I personally would like to read. While it's always a joy to find other readers who enjoy the stories I do, I'm aware my brand of writing won't please everyone. Please, write to me anyway. I'd love to hear from you. Gail@gaildaley.com

Honest reviews are critical to all authors, but especially critical to Indie authors like myself, so please take a few minutes to tell me what you think of my work. It would be much appreciated if you write a review and share it on the site where you purchased it. Reviews don't have to be long and analytical. Just say what you think as though chatting with a friend. On behalf of all Indie writers and publishers PLEASE, ALWAYS WRITE A REVIEW for any book you read or audiobook you listen to.

If you would like to know when my next books are coming out, please follow me on social media sites or sign up to receive E-mail notices, either through Books2Read: https://books2read.com/author/gail-daley/subscribe/1/72820/

Or directly on my website: https://gaildaley.com/Sign-Up-4-Newsletters.php

A copy of my privacy policy can be found on https://gaildaley.com/Privacy-Policy.php

BONUS: EXCERPT FROM APEX PREDATOR

HEIRS OF AVALON — BOOK 2 THE
OUTLAW COLONIES

APEX

PREDATOR

THE OUTLAWED COLONIES

3

GAIL DALEY

GAIL DALEY

COPYRIGHT

E-BOOK ISBN: 978-1-68564-017-0
PB ISBN- 978-1-68564-018-7

HB ISBN 978-1-68489-198-6

ASIN:

For permission requests, write to the publisher, addressed "Attention: Permissions Coordinator," at the address below.
Gail Daley
5688 E Sussex Way
Fresno, CA 93727
www.gaildaley.com

ABOUT THIS BOOK

The first world discovered by the Laughing Mountain Scientists was a doozy. A fitting match for Homo Sapiens—the deadliest predator of all time—maybe.

If the native animals here don't get you, the plants just might.

Life is hard on the outlaw colony of Lemuria. Some days it's a struggle to stay alive. The plants and animals are huge and deadly. Homo Sapiens are apex predators, but they may have met their match on this planet.

Zach Tylor is young, tough, and broke. He needs the money, so despite his better judgement, he agrees to guide a group of researchers to a mysterious structure the colonists called the Halivaara Wheel. During the trip, he uncovers a dangerous conspiracy that threatens not only his home planet, but all the Outlawed Colonies.

HUNTING VARMITS

A WHUFFLING snort in his ear woke Zach Tylor from a sound sleep. He turned his head to find a pig-like snout about an inch from his nose. The snout belonged to Lucy, his semi-guard pet. The scientific name for Lucy's species was Lupinus Leo. Colonists referred to them as Banded Koodoo. Zach just called her Lucy. Lucy's DNA said she had both feline and canine characteristics; she had the retractable claws and night vision of a cat and the devotion and loyalty of a dog. She stood eighteen inches high at the shoulders and weighed about sixty pounds, with coarse, oily, red fur, broken by horizontal yellow stripes along her back and tail. She had short, pricked ears and large dark eyes. Spines made of the same substance as her claws ran up and down her back as a predator defense. Her tail, wide at the base, narrowed to a barbed ball at the end.

She was regarding him with the alert attention that told him she wanted a human to fix what was wrong. The ambient light in the room told Zach it was about an hour before dawn. It was too early for his brood of Sun Risers, the large fluffy birds he kept for their meat, eggs, and feathers, to be awake unless something was bothering them. Since he didn't hear the restless clucking signaling they were alarmed, he decided whatever had prompted Lucy to wake him wasn't bothering the Sun Risers.

He slid out of bed, wincing when his bare feet hit the icy floor. The stone left by the aliens who had built his house was smooth, but it was also cold. He pulled on his leather pants and shoved his feet into his high-topped boots. The shirt was from the night before, but he had

only worn it two days, so he considered it clean enough to hunt varmints.

Grabbing his night-vision enabled helmet and his pulse rifle, he stepped outside into the inner Bailey inside the high walls made of iridescent stone left by the Aliens enclosing his garden. The area had no roof, but the walls were tall enough to keep out most of Lemuria's larger predators and wandering herbivore herds. Generally, the walls kept his vegetable garden and the bird coop safe from predators. He had built a fence with access to his Elfs and Raffe corrals and sheds on one end of the Bailey. The exterior corrals also had high walls, but the end open to the valley was edged with a more modern contrivance—a shock fence.

Elfs were draft animals, as large as earthly elephants, with long wooly coats that could be sheared and woven into cloth. Both bulls and cows

possessed sharp tusks which usually
provided all the protection a herd
needed. Like the elephants they had
been nicknamed after, they also had
a long prehensile trunk with long
fingery appendages on the end. It
served as a nose and occasionally a
hand. Their wide ears hung from the
tops of their heads and helped
protect their eyes and faces.

The Raffe's were riding animals;
tall, spindly legged critters with
triangle shaped heads set on their
long necks, a smooth, straight back
that would hold a saddle if it was
fastened on with chest and rump
straps in addition to the cinch.

Both herds were quiet, although
the Raffes were restless, but they
always were. He glanced at Lucy. She
was staring at the garden.

Zach stopped and stood still about
thirty yards from his garden. Even
with the night-vision visor, it
required concentration to

distinguish shapes. Lucy whined and his hand dropped to her head, a signal to be quiet.

It was more of those bloody Coney Rats. The Coney Rats were the scourge of Lemuria's farmers. They ran in large family groups and could clear a crop field in a few hours. Smaller than Lucy, the Coney Rats were no match for her individually, but in a horde, they could beat her senseless. They weren't actually rats, being genetically closer to earthly rabbits. The Coneys had excellent tasting meat, and a strong, thick skin, covered in long fluffy hair which could be scraped and woven into light cloth suitable for summer clothing.

He took aim with his rifle and downed six of the invaders before they realized he was shooting at them. He got six more as the horde leaped for the fence to escape. Their powerful back legs easily allowing them to jump to the top. He got several more as the horde went over the high wall in a wave. The rising sun hitting the top of the wall silhouetted the rodents, making them easy targets.

By the time Zach had collected his bounty, ensured any survivors passed into the ether, and hung the carcasses in his butcher shed under stasis to keep until he had time to deal with processing the meat, the Sun Risers were griping to be let out and fed.

He opened the coop, and a dozen or so of the balls of fiery colored fluff bounced out. The sheer mass of the Ball of bright feathers on each bird not only made excellent decorative items, but their feathers also made it hard for predators to tell where their plumages ended, and the bird's body began. Unwary predators often came up with a mouthful of fluff instead of a piece of bird anatomy.

Zach scattered some cracked corn for them and went to turn off the shock fence so the Raffes and Elfs could graze in the area just outside the compound.

He was looking forward to eating breakfast when the com link chimed. Hastily running his fingers through his tangled mane of dark hair, he answered it.

The woman on the other end was Terella van Horn. Among other things, the van Horn's handled the insertion of new-commers into Lemurian society and had been instrumental in stopping the revolt that nearly captured the portal last year. The van Horns, like Zach's family the Tylor's, were one of Lemuria's Founding Families. Although Lemuria was the first world the town of Laughing Mountain discovered able to support human life, it had been a hard sell until

the Alien Ruins had been found. On
earth there existed a group of people
who believed Aliens had visited earth
in the distant past, but they hadn't
found much actual evidence to prove
it. Laughing Mountain was willing to
sell access to Lemuria if the
proposed colonists were willing to
never attempt to publish their
findings on earth. If Earth's Portal
Authority had discovered the
existence of a gate leading to an
unauthorized world, it would have
destroyed the colony and the town
which ran the illegal Portal, so the
terms of the sale had included a non-
disclosure clause.

Although not as well financed as
the planned colonies of Barsoom,
Arcadia, and Shangri-La, the Founding
Families who made up the first two
hundred Lemurian colonists were an
organized group of historians and
scientists who pooled their money to
purchase farming, mining, and

communication equipment to send through the Portal. They also invested in seeds for crops and weapons for defense against the large animals already inhabiting the planet.

To survive Lemuria's predatory plants and animals, the Founding Families realized they needed to learn to work together fusing their interests to become a community. Since the first arrivals, other colonists had trickled through the Portal, and the original society had become somewhat fractured, but the laws and government created by those first families had held up well.

Terella was a few years younger than Zach. She always presented the fresh, button-downed picture of a sophisticated academic. Her white-blond hair was drawn back in a neat twist, showing off her fine-boned face with its generous, wide lipped mouth and dark grey eyes. Today she

wore a pale pink blouse, demurely buttoned up to her slim neck and a pair of dark grey trousers. For some reason that prim air attracted Zach; he always had the urge to grab her and physically mess it up.

He wished fervently he had had time to shower and shave before she called. Ruefully, he put the wish aside and got down to business; Terella wouldn't have called him unless she had a job for him.

"What can I do for you, Miss van Horn?" he asked.

"Are you up for a guide job?" she asked.

'I might be," he said cautiously, swiftly calculating the amount of money he had locked up in his hidden safe. If the job paid enough, the extra money might mean he could enclose the lower end of the valley to plant several fields. "Who is it for and how much does it pay?"

Terella smiled at him. He was entirely unaware of the masculine impact he made on women, even needing a shave and grubby from lack of sleep and collecting Coney Rat corpses. His blood-spattered tee shirt clung tightly to his brawny shoulders and chest. Corded muscles in his powerful biceps and forearms stuck out of the sleeves.

"It's a family of newcomers," she said. "A Professor and Mrs. Lamont. They have two kids, a boy about thirteen and a girl about sixteen. They want to go out to the Halivaara Wheel by the Scarlet Lagoon."

Before colonists had arrived on Lemuria, a mapping drone had explored the planet. Topographical printouts of its findings were stored in the Government House Library. There were no recognized trails through the Duranga Savana, the prairie between the town, the Faraway Mountains to the north and the Shimmering Ocean to

the south. The Halivaara Wheel had
shown up next to the Scarlet Lagoon
as several large circles of the
Alien's iridescent material with
spokes leading from the center and
connecting the outlying circles.
Unlike the smaller ruins left by the
aliens, an estimate of its size was
nearly seventeen kilometers, nearly
three times as large as any other
settlement found.

If they made it to the Wheel,
Lamont's expedition would be the
first to reach it. Despite the
yearning to find and explore anything
left by the Alien Forerunners, the
planet itself had made concentrating
on anything but survival difficult.
An earlier attempt to reach the
Halivaara Wheel in a dirigible
aircraft, had come to grief when the
vessel was attacked by a pair of
Harlequin Dragons. Harlequin Dragons
were about half the size of the
dirigible, but their attack damaged

it, creating a large hole allowing the gas keeping it in the air to escape. It was forced to land before it crashed. Unfortunately, the explorers who had risked everything had no more money to build a second dirigible or repair the damaged craft, so they limped back into Shellgate several months later.

Harlequin Dragons bore some resemblance to the descriptions of those found in earthly myths, hence the name, but they were Avians, with contrasting tiny feathers in patterns of red, black, and turquoise on their heads, necks, wings, and chests.

"How new are they?" Zach asked suspiciously. Bear Leading newcomers through the hostile area to the site could be difficult.

"Pretty new," Terella admitted. "He's willing to pay." She named a price high enough to enable Zach to enclose the field and still have a little left over.

"What's the catch?" Zach asked. "For that price the guides in town will be falling over themselves to take it on. Why me?"

"Some of them might abandon the Lamont's in the middle of the journey. He's—arrogant. I know if you take the job, you'll stick to it."

Zach translated this: the man was a jerk who didn't take orders.

"Uh—huh." He named a price half again over what she had quoted. They dickered for a few minutes, finally settling on a price that included feed for himself and his animals and paying for a crew to help with the travel and outfit the expedition, as well as a bonus for aggravation.

"I'll see you in a few hours," he told her. "I have some arrangements to make here first. If he and I can't come to an agreement, I get a deposit for coming in to meet him," he warned her.

"Of course," she said.

Ten minutes later with his unruly hair tied back and wearing a cleaner shirt, he headed out the door. On the way out he grabbed a couple of smoked meat strips for himself and Lucy to eat on the way.

When he fired up his two-seater airsled, Lucy, her mouth full of meat, jumped aboard.

As an afterthought, he also grabbed the new hooded cape he had recently finished weaving. He was especially proud of the workmanship; he had dyed strands of Coney thread in brilliant shades of blue and green and woven them into a shimmery blanket of color which rippled with movement. He was sure Mrs. Smithers would want it for her daughter Dulcia, whom she was anxious to marry off. He intended to offer it to her in exchange for young Jimmy's services in taking care of his garden and animals while he was gone.

The Smither's family were long
time neighbors. Her first husband had
been Zach's cousin James. James had
been killed by a pack of Crested
wolves. Zach considered himself an
uncle to the two children Dulcia and
Jimmy.

Mrs. Smithers, a slatternly woman
with fading red hair, had once been
pretty but the years had been hard,
and her looks had faded. Now she
concentrated her ambitions on finding
a husband for her sixteen-year-old
daughter. Because she considered Zach
an ideal catch despite the kinship
issue, he always dealt cautiously
with her—wary of falling into one of
her matrimonial honey traps.

Today the trap was relatively easy
to dodge; when she mentioned Dulcia
joining him on the expedition as a
cook, he simply said, "I'm sorry, but
I only negotiated payment for myself.
You'll have to speak to Terella van
Horn about that." Not true but he

knew if he admitted he had already negotiated for a cook's wages, Joann Smithers would keep the entire amount of Dulcia's wages for herself.

He dropped young Jimmy off at his farm, grabbed a spare bedroll and more smoked meat and headed back out with Lucy again riding shotgun.

Airsleds on Lemuria were powered by an esoteric energy crystal found only on the planet. A machine blueprint etched on the wall of one of the mysterious quartz buildings had been built by an enterprising engineer named Mikhailovich Gregor. He went looking for the crystals shown on the design and found them purely by chance (he tripped and fell into a cave). The cave showed evidence that it had been mined at one time. He dug a few out and tried them in his new engine. No one was more surprised than himself when the engine produced power. He named the Crystals Lechatelierites but

everyone else called them Gregor's
Crystals.

The motor built by the engineer
was too large to be portable.
However, a Portal Runner who also
frequented Barsoom, another of the
outlaw colonies saw the design. Upon
hearing it worked, he hunted up
Gregor and proposed letting the
scientists on Barsoom, who
specialized in miniaturized
robotics, have a go at developing a
smaller version.

Barsoom's scientists were
successful, Gregor and the Runner got
rich, and versions of the X-T motor
were now used to run most of the
machines used on Lemuria. The crystal
and the Mikhailovich Engine had
garnered interest on Arcadia as well,
and the enterprising Arcadians were
attempting to develop a Portal going
directly from their colony to Lemuria
to facilitate mining the crystal.
There wasn't enough storage space in

the Portal town of Laughing Mountain for the quantity of Crystals the Arcadians want, so a direct gateway from Lemuria to Arcadia made sense.

The sled made the fifty-mile trip to Shellgate, the colony capital, in less than two hours. Shellgate City was the only large settlement on Lemuria. It boasted a population of about five thousand people including residents and transients.

As Zach topped the rise leading into the valley towards the city, he could see the cluster of government buildings and the stone arch in the center square. The colonists had unconsciously copied the Architectural style of the Forerunners. Streets led away from the arch and government buildings like the spokes of a wagon wheel. Shellgate itself was a unique assortment of styles, a mixed bag of prefabricated buildings and native stone or wood. Raffes and Elfs mixed freely on the streets with bicycles, tricycles, and air sleds.

Zach stopped at the Red Cat Tavern on his way to the government center. His friend Marley Redfern owned it and would usually keep one of the upstairs rooms free for him if he knew Zach was in town.

He was in luck; Marley had a free room. "Jace is cooking up roasted Ibex and we're serving it with a mess of fried tubers and red beans," Marley said. "Try to be here for dinner—you don't want to miss it."

Terella had commed Zach on his way into town. "Is there something going on with you and Dulcia Smithers?" she asked,

"Good God No!" he exclaimed. "The kid is what—sixteen?"

"Her mother seems to think so," she said, watching him with her head cocked to one side.

"Dulcia and her brother are my cousin James' kids. I'm the only family left on his side, so I feel sort of responsible for them. Her mother," he said with emphasis, "has been trying to marry that poor kid off since she was thirteen!"

"Oh, dear," Terella said. "She wants me to hire Dulcia as a cook. Do you want me to turn her down?"

He sighed. "Dulcia is a good cook. She wants to earn enough to escape from her mom. She won't be a problem. I explained the situation to her the last time her mother tried to get her to crawl into my bed. She was embarrassed, but she did understand I don't have sex with children."

"She was lucky it was someone like you, not some jerk who would have taken advantage of her." Terella said.

"You'll have to give Joann Smithers a portion of Dulcia's wages

but set some of them aside for the
kid."

"I can do that."

She closed the com as Zach pulled
up in front of the Government house.
Leaving Lucy to guard the sled, he
entered the two-story building.
Outside the building had been slapped
together with prefab material and it
showed. Inside someone had tried to
improve the look with paint. Art from
local artists was scattered around
the large foyer.

Zach nodded at the receptionist
and went down the hall to Terella's
office.

She was perched in her chair
behind the heavy wooden desk,
obviously attempting to soothe the
family of newcomers sitting on a
leather covered couch. The man was
tall and spare, with a neat goatee
and a pair of black framed glasses
perched on his beak of a nose. His
wife was of similar height and build,

with her hair drawn back in a tight bun. She was dressed in a neat suit dress. The two children both wore earth issue clothing. The boy Herve' a lad of about thirteen, was dressed in cargo pants and a tee-shirt in virulent colors. He was a little overweight, with sandy hair and a pale complexion, denoting a sedentary lifestyle. The daughter, Josette, looked about sixteen. She wore a low-cut tank top and skintight leggings. She also wore a pair of flip flop shoes.

"Ah—you made it," Terella smiled brightly at Zach. "Zach, this is Professor and Mrs. Lamont, and their children, Herve' and Josette. Professor, this is Zachery Tylor, one of our best guides."

"I still don't see why we need a guide," Lamont griped. "I've seen a map of the area. It's due north from here. With a good compass, there is no way we can get lost."

"Getting lost isn't the danger," Zach said.

"Yes, there are hazards on the way to the site you aren't familiar with," Terella said.

"Can I see the supply list?" Zach asked.

When Terella handed it over, he went through it carefully, marking through a few lines and writing more at the bottom. He handed it back to her and she passed it to the Professor, who scanned it with an ever-increasing frown.

Zach looked them over while the Professor read his corrections. Many newcomers were under the impression the rules here were the same as those on earth. Most of them also discounted the non-disclosure/non-publish Law about their findings on Lemuria; it was illegal to reveal anything concerning Lemuria or the other colonies back on earth. On Lemuria, the penalty for attempting

to violate this law was a long term in a labor camp for a first offense. A second offense rated the death penalty.

Even if colonists proved the existence of X-T visitors, it wouldn't change that law. Lemuria, the Laughing Mountain Portal, and the other Outlaw colonies *needed* earth to remain in ignorance of their existence.

Second and third generation colonists were aware of the penalties for breaking the Non-Disclosure Law, but most of the colonists were so desperately poor they were willing to assist newcomers in their research anyway as it put much needed coin in their pockets.

The Professor waived his corrected sheet of supplies at Zach. "These items are necessary," he said. "We need them to operate efficiently."

"Those items aren't available on Lemuria," Zach said patiently.

"Young man, you don't understand.
I insist this expedition be equipped
with top-of-the-line instruments."

"I'm sorry," Zach said. "But
unless you brought them with you, it
isn't possible to obtain them here."

"So, order them from earth. I
don't see the problem. I assure you
our sponsors will ship them
promptly."

Zach and Terella regarded the two
newcomers with pity. "Did you read
the Non-Disclosure Clause in your
immigration contract?" Zach asked.

"Yes, of course, but surely that
is only a formality—"

He stopped when Zach shook his
head no, "I'm afraid it *isn't* a
formality. It's a very real fact." He
turned to Terella, "Perhaps you could
refresh their memories?"

Terella nodded and withdrew two
pamphlets out of her desk drawer,
handing one to the Lamonts. She
opened hers to read the contract

aloud. Zach, who could probably have recited the entire short volume from memory, leaned against the wall with his arms crossed and listened in silence.

'I, the undersigned, agree to have no further contact with earth or its population in any form whatsoever for any reason.

I understand this is a one-way passage and I will not attempt to return to earth or contact anyone there.

Moneys received from any earth source will be funneled through channels that do not reveal the presence of the Lemuria colony or Laughing Mountain's involvement with the colony.

Any of my findings gained from exploring Lemuria can only be published in the Colony of Lemuria.'

"I have the colony copy of the contract with your signatures on

file. I can furnish you with another
if you've lost yours."

Professor Lamont sat down limply
in a chair. His wife had tears
running down her face.

"Richard what are we going to do?"
she whispered.

Terella went to the file cabinet
and took their actual contract out of
the 'to be filed' box.

"According to this, you will
continue to receive a yearly salary
from earth, so you won't starve. A
sufficient sum of money has been
deposited into an account in your
name to enable you to live
comfortably for a year and to equip
an expedition to study the alien
ruins. If the payments continue as
scheduled, they will support you long
enough for you to establish
yourselves."

Lamont looked up sharply. "What do
you mean 'if they continue'? Why
wouldn't they continue?"

Terella hesitated before she said, "Judging from experience, after a few years, Earth organizations who sent researchers here usually stop funding an expedition from which they gain nothing."

"That doesn't make sense," Alice Lamont protested. "Why send us here at all if they know we can't report what we find?"

"There could be any number of reasons for that Mrs. Lamont," Terella said kindly. "It's better to concentrate on getting you settled so you can make some decisions about your future, than to waste time speculating on the reasons you were sent here."

"What about the expedition? Is it still on?" Zach asked.

"That will depend on Professor and Mrs. Lamont. However, the deposit is non-refundable; you and the others will be paid for your time and trouble."

"What?" Lamont exclaimed. "Why should they get paid for an expedition that doesn't take place?"

"Our laws in respect to these matters may be different than those on earth," Terella said. "Once the offer has been posted, those who signed up for employment under its offer are considered hired. If the expedition is cancelled, they are entitled to severance pay to cover time and wages lost."

She looked up as her younger brother Terrence poked his head in the door. "I have rooms arranged for the Lamonts at Mrs. Riker's boarding house," he said.

"Excellent. Why don't you go and settle into your rooms, have a meal and we'll discuss this further tomorrow." Gently but inexorably, she guided them to the door, shutting it behind them.

"Are you staying at Marley's?" she asked.

Zach nodded. "He said he has a spare bed. Why don't you join me for dinner? He sets a good table."

"Maybe I will if I get done in time. About seven?"

"Sure." He watched the engrossing sway of her hips in the tight jeans as she walked away from him.

Want to read more? Click here https://books2read.com/u/4ELPxY

CPSIA information can be obtained
at www.ICGtesting.com
Printed in the USA
LVHW042103150922
728494LV00004B/30